"There's no reason for you to sleep on the couch,"

Gillian said. "You're obviously uncomfortable."

"If you've come to offer me the daybed, forget it. It isn't any longer than this couch," Taggart replied.

"I'm giving you *my* bed. The daybed fits me just fine," she said, frowning. "Besides, you're difficult enough to get along with when you aren't grouchy. If you sleep on that couch and get a backache or a cramp in your neck, you'll be impossible."

"Go to bed, Gillian."

"*I'm* going to sleep on the daybed. *You* can sleep wherever you please."

He smiled.

Dear Reader,

What's a single FABULOUS FATHER to do when he discovers he has another daughter—a child he never knew about? Why, marry the secretive mom, of course! And that's exactly what he proposes in Moyra Tarling's *Twice a Father*. Don't miss this wonderful story.

This month, two authors celebrate the publication of their twenty-fifth Silhouette books! *A Handy Man To Have Around* is Elizabeth August's twenty-fifth book—and part of her bestselling miniseries, SMYTHESHIRE, MASSACHUSETTS. In this delightful novel, a tall, dark and gorgeous hunk sure proves to be A Handy Man To Have Around when a small-town gal needs big-time help!

Daddy on the Run is Carla Cassidy's twenty-fifth book for Silhouette—and part of her intriguing miniseries THE BAKER BROOD. In this heartwarming tale, a married dad can finally come home—to his waiting wife and daughter.

In Toni Collins's *Willfully Wed*, a sexy private investigator learns who anonymously left a lovely lady a potful of money. But telling the truth could break both their hearts!

Denied his child for years, a single dad wants his son—*and* the woman caring for the boy—in *Substitute Mom* by Maris Soule.

And finally, there's only one thing a bachelor cop with a baby on his hands can do: call for maternal backup in Cara Colter's *Baby in Blue*.

Six wonderful love stories by six talented authors—that's what you'll find this and every month in Silhouette Romance!

Enjoy every one...

Melissa Senate
Senior Editor

Please address questions and book requests to:
Silhouette Reader Service
U.S.: 3010 Walden Ave., P.O. Box 1325, Buffalo, NY 14269
Canadian: P.O. Box 609, Fort Erie, Ont. L2A 5X3

ELIZABETH AUGUST

A HANDY MAN TO HAVE AROUND

Silhouette
ROMANCE™
Published by Silhouette Books
America's Publisher of Contemporary Romance

To Sondra and Kenny...two of the warmest,
most caring people I know.

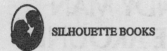

SILHOUETTE BOOKS

ISBN 0-373-19157-X

A HANDY MAN TO HAVE AROUND

Copyright © 1996 by Elizabeth August

This edition published by arrangement with Harlequin Books S.A.

® and TM are trademarks of Harlequin Books S.A., used under license.
Trademarks indicated with ® are registered in the United States Patent
and Trademark Office, the Canadian Trade Marks Office and in other
countries.

Printed in U.S.A.

Books by Elizabeth August

ELIZABETH AUGUST

"*A Handy Man To Have Around* is my 25th book for Silhouette! I began writing romances the year my youngest son was born. He is now a junior in high school. My eldest son is in his last year of medical school and my middle son is in his fourth year of college. And, this year, my husband and I will celebrate our 29th wedding anniversary.

"I want to thank you, the readers of romance, with all my heart. Without you I would not be able to pursue this career, which has brought me so much pleasure."

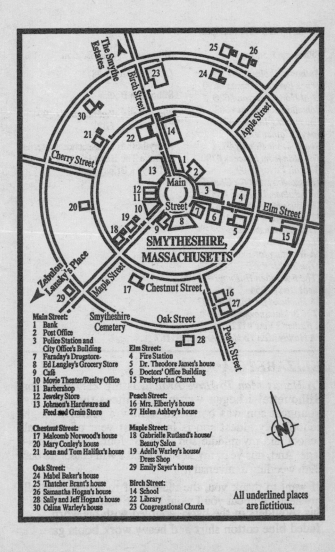

SMYTHESHIRE, MASSACHUSETTS

The Smythe Estates

Birch Street

Apple Street

25   26

24

23

30

21   22   14

Cherry Street

13   1   2

Main Street   3   4

12   Elm Street
11   6   5
10   7
19   8
18   9   15

20

Zebulon Lansky's Place

29

Maple Street

17   Chestnut Street

16
27

Smytheshire Cemetery

Oak Street

28

Peach Street

N

Main Street:
1 Bank
2 Post Office
3 Police Station and
   City Office's Building
7 Faraday's Drugstore
8 Ed Langley's Grocery Store
9 Café
10 Movie Theater/Realty Office
11 Barbershop
12 Jewelry Store
13 Johnson's Hardware and
   Feed and Grain Store

Chestnut Street:
17 Malcomb Norwood's house
20 Mary Conley's house
21 Joan and Tom Halifax's house

Oak Street:
24 Mabel Baker's house
25 Thatcher Brant's house
26 Samantha Hogan's house
28 Sally and Jeff Hogan's house
30 Celina Warley's house

Elm Street:
4 Fire Station
5 Dr. Theodore James's house
6 Doctors' Office Building
15 Presbyterian Church

Peach Street:
16 Mrs. Elberly's house
27 Helen Ashbey's house

Maple Street:
18 Gabrielle Rutland's house/
   Beauty Salon
19 Adelle Warley's house/
   Dress Shop
29 Emily Sayer's house

Birch Street:
14 School
22 Library
23 Congregational Church

All underlined places
are fictitious.

Chapter One

Gillian Hudson's hand closed into a fist, crumpling the letter she was holding. Only moments ago, she'd been thinking about how, after two years of living in this small town tucked away in the mountains of northwestern Massachusetts, she was actually beginning to relax and feel safe once again. But that had been before she'd gotten back from her errands and found the white, business-size envelope lying on her desk.

Her knuckles whitened against the cheap piece of lined, yellow paper. No. This couldn't be happening to her!

"Bad news?"

Gillian jerked around to see Taggart Devereux in the study doorway. The handyman's muscular, six-foot-two-inch bulk seemed to fill the entrance to the room. His black hair, shaggy around the ears and hanging nearly to his shoulders in the back, coupled with his worn jeans, faded blue cotton shirt and heavy work boots gave him the appearance of the stereotypical stoic, insular mountain man. And, as far as she could determine, he was.

Wanda Elberly, Gillian's grandaunt, to whom this house belonged, had hired him to repaint the entire place. For the past couple of days, he'd been there from dawn to dusk, and Gillian could count on one hand the number of words he'd spoken to her during that time. Even his business conversations with her grandaunt were held to a minimum.

"You look like you're going to faint." He took a step toward her and added dryly, "Never pictured you as the fainting type."

"I'm not." With a cool look, she stopped his approach. She'd been standing beside her desk. Now, with a dignity that belied the weakness in her legs, she seated herself.

A cat's angry mew split the air. Looking like a sulking tiger woken from his afternoon sleep, Tom, the huge old yellow cat, who considered himself master of this house, stalked past the study door.

"Something's terribly wrong!" a frantic, elderly voice exclaimed from the hall. In the next instant, Wanda Elberly brushed past Taggart and hobbled arthritically into the room. "My crystals are making the most horrendous racket. Reminds me of a badly tuned string quartet all trying to play a different song." She glanced over her shoulder toward the door. "They've certainly gotten Tom riled. He doesn't like to be disturbed when he's sleeping."

Gillian saw Taggart give her grandaunt an indulgent glance. She knew it was the general consensus of the fifteen hundred residents of Smytheshire that a faulty connection in the elderly woman's hearing aids was what caused her to think she heard a range of musical sounds emitting from her collection of geodes and crystals. Gillian cocked an eyebrow toward Taggart, silently calling him a cynic, then turned her attention to her grandaunt. "I simply received an unpleasant letter."

Wanda's eyes widened. "Not—" she began, only to clamp her mouth shut when she realized she and her grandniece were not alone.

Gillian's hand had gone numb. She forced it open, and the letter fell to the floor. Before she could retrieve it, the handyman picked it up. She made a grab for it, but he took a step back, evading her reach.

Stretching the paper out, he read it. His usual indifferent expression turned to one of disgust. "You get a lot of mail like this?"

"No." A scarlet flush tinted her cheeks, and she snatched the letter from him.

"Since everyone else is getting a look, I'd like a peek myself." Wanda extended her hand.

"You really don't want to read this trash." Gillian folded the letter with the intent of returning it to the envelope. She wanted to throw it away, but past experience had taught her that could be foolish.

"I'm too old to be shocked." Wanda clasped the edge of the letter between her thumb and finger and gave it a mild jerk.

Knowing how persistent the elderly woman could be, Gillian relented. She watched her grandaunt's face as Wanda read the first sentence. It proclaimed that Gillian and the letter writer should be performing a particular scene together. Next came a page clipped from one of Gillian's books in which the hero and heroine were making love. Beneath that the writer promised that one day he and Gillian would know this kind of passion.

"Ardent admirer my foot!" Wanda snapped, reading the sender's chosen appellation aloud. "Sick pervert is more like it!"

Out of the corner of her eye, Gillian saw the stack of mail she'd just brought back from the post office and a chill raced through her. When she moved to Smytheshire, she'd attempted to insulate herself from the rest of the world. One of her ploys had been to take a post office box in Griswoldville, a town several miles away. But this letter had not been among those she'd just carried in. Grabbing the envelope in which the offensive letter had arrived, she read the address printed in stiff, precise penmanship. "He knows where I live," she gasped out around the lump of panic in her throat.

Wanda's eyes rounded in shock. "That's the letter I put on your desk?"

"I'm calling Thatcher Brant." Taggart reached for the phone. "Have you got a phone book in here?"

Terrifying memories played through Gillian's mind. "The police can't do anything until someone gets hurt."

Taggart had been scanning the top of the desk for the phone book. Now he paused to study her narrowly. "This has happened to you before?"

"A friend. It happened to a friend," Gillian replied, her complexion ashen.

"Thatcher needs to know. Where's the phone book?" Taggart demanded.

Opening the top drawer of her desk, Gillian produced the magazine-size volume. "Calling the police won't do any good," she repeated, as Taggart looked up the number and dialed.

"Well, it can't hurt," Wanda said, giving Taggart a nod of approval.

A few minutes later, the three of them were gathered in the living room with Chief of Police Thatcher Brant.

Gillian glanced toward a table set in front of one of the windows. Wanda's geodes and crystals covered nearly the entire surface. Normally the sun would be reflecting off of them, causing them to glitter and cast spots of rainbow reflections on the walls and ceiling. But, at the moment, Wanda had them covered with a velvet cloth to muffle the sounds that were disturbing her. Gillian supposed that was just as well. Still, she missed their cheerful sparkle.

Taggart had remained standing, leaning against the doorjamb, while Wanda, Gillian and Thatcher were seated in the chair and couch grouping surrounding the antique coffee table in the center of the room. Thatcher Brant had read the letter and was now studying the envelope.

"It's postmarked Seattle, Washington," he noted. "I'll call the police there and see if they have anyone in their files who likes to send these kind of letters."

Gillian's attention returned to the policeman, and she nodded. The tall, muscular, brown-haired police chief had a manner that normally inspired confidence. But her memories of the past were too strong. "Even if you do discover who sent this, all I can do is get a court order that requires him to not communicate with me further and stay fifty or a hundred feet away from me at all times."

Thatcher raised a questioning eyebrow. "You've been through this before?"

"A friend of mine. Another romance writer." Ida Hyatt's face filled Gillian's mind. The pretty, vivacious blonde was laughing, then there was a scream. Gillian's gaze locked onto the police chief's. "She started getting letters. The police were able to find out who the man was. His name was Clyde Halley, a real loner, no friends, and his family didn't want to have anything to do with him. He'd been arrested several times as a Peeping Tom. She got a restraining order. He got mad and ran her down with his car. I was there. I was hit, too, but I was lucky. I spent four months in the hospital and ended up with a few scars, but I have my life."

"What happened to the man?" Taggart asked.

Gillian turned to him. His expression was the usual cool, aloof one she'd grown used to seeing. Then her eyes met his and in those midnight blue depths was a protectiveness that caused her to feel as if she was being enfolded in a warm blanket. Startled, for a moment she couldn't speak. Then the images of the past reappeared and cold reality returned. "He wrote a note saying he didn't want to live if Ida was dead, then he shot himself."

"If you don't mind, I'll take this letter with me." Thatcher picked up the envelope, drawing her attention back to him. "If you get any more, handle them as little as possible and call me immediately. In the meantime, I'll pass the word around that I want to know of any strangers in town."

A shiver traveled along Gillian's spine. "I don't understand how he found me. I'm not listed in the phone book. Since I left California, I've had my publisher's address used as the one fans should send letters to. Even my agent and editor only have my post office box in Griswoldville as an address."

"If a person is looking for someone, there are always ways of finding them. I assume you put your grandaunt's address on your driver's license. And your parents and other relatives know where you're living. They might have inadvertently given out that information. Then there's a lot of people in town who know you're the Gillian Hudson who writes the romance novels. One of them might have mentioned knowing you."

Gillian knew Thatcher was right. Besides, how the letter writer had gotten her address no longer mattered. He had it.

Thatcher smiled encouragingly. "Don't worry. No stranger can arrive in town unnoticed."

Gillian nodded, but knowing this was so wasn't a reassurance.

"I'll see the chief to the door," Taggart volunteered, easing himself into a straightened position.

As soon as the men were gone, Gillian turned to her grandaunt. "I can't stay here."

Wanda took her hand and gave it a squeeze. "What you can't do is run like a frightened rabbit every time some lunatic scribbles a bit of nonsense on a piece of paper."

"I don't want to leave. I've grown to like it here," Gillian confessed. "But I can't stay and risk you getting hurt because of me."

"You're safer here than you'd be anywhere else. No stranger is going to set foot in Smytheshire without us knowing about it," Wanda argued.

Gillian shook her head. "No, I have to go. I won't risk your safety."

"If you're looking for a place to hide out for a while, you can come up to my cabin. I've got a couple of hunting dogs who'll let you know if anyone's around."

Gillian turned to see Taggart standing in the doorway. He reminded her of granite. The thought that, if she were looking for a bodyguard, he would be an excellent choice played through her mind.

"Gillian can't go traipsing off to your place," Wanda scolded. "Think what people would say. She'd have no reputation left."

"I wasn't offering to bed her. I was merely offering her sanctuary," Taggart drawled, again leaning against the doorjamb.

Gillian felt the sting of insult. Granted, for the past couple of years she hadn't put any effort into making herself look attractive. She had, in fact, attempted to fade into the background as much as possible. But her features were well formed. And she'd always considered her hickory-brown eyes an asset. Of course there was her hair. Long, straight and a rather plain brown, it was hanging in a nondescript style that did give her a dowdy look. And her clothing wasn't any better. There had been a time when she'd turned a few heads with her curvaceous figure. Now she kept it hidden beneath baggy shirts and loose-fitting slacks. And still, a nut had singled her out!

"Well, the gossips of this town won't think the two of you are simply having a platonic relationship," Wanda retorted.

Gillian was again recalling the car coming at her and Ida. "I appreciate the offer, Taggart, but my grandaunt's right." Rising abruptly, she started to the door. "I've got to pack."

"You can't just run," Wanda protested again.

"I can't stay," Gillian shot back over her shoulder.

Suddenly Taggart blocked her exit. "Wanda's right. You could find yourself running into more trouble than you're running away from."

Gillian glared up at him. "This isn't easy for me, but I know what I have to do."

"Looks to me like you're reacting out of fear instead of thinking this out clearly," he cautioned.

"You haven't spoken a handful of words to me in all the time you've been working in this house. In fact, you haven't spoken a handful of words to me in all the time I've been here in Smytheshire, and now suddenly you think you're an expert on me and how I should live my life. I think not! Now get out of my way, please."

Taggart didn't move. "I'm not claiming to be an expert on you. My daddy didn't raise a fool. I'd never claim to be an expert on any woman. But I do know something about hunting. The fastest and surest way to get your prey is to flush them out. If they stay quiet, they're less likely to be caught."

"I've already been found!"

"But you have the home advantage. He can't sneak up on you here."

"You listen to Taggart. The man makes sense," Wanda said, rising and approaching them.

"How many letters did your friend get before her 'admirer' decided to get nasty?" Taggart asked.

"Several, ten, I think," Gillian replied.

"Then it seems to me you've got a little time to think about what your next move should be."

Gillian had to admit he was probably right.

"It could be that this lunatic will only send the one letter and then forget about you," Wanda suggested hopefully. "Maybe he gets a kick out of shaking up romance writers. If you ask around, you might find that several have received similar letters."

"I have heard of others getting off-color letters that were of no consequence," Gillian conceded.

"There, you see." Wanda nodded vigorously. "Now I don't want to hear any more nonsense about you taking flight."

Gillian's panic subsided enough for her to analyze the situation. They were right. Fleeing in whatever direction the wind took her wasn't the answer. "All right. I'll take a couple of days to think about what I should do."

Wanda smiled triumphantly. "We'll see this through together."

That wasn't an option, Gillian countered silently. She would not risk her grandaunt's safety. But she was in no mood for any further argument at the moment. Turning to the door, she discovered Taggart still blocked the doorway. "I've agreed to stick around for a little while. Now, may I go? I've got some writing I need to do."

For a moment he looked as if he had more to say, then his expression became shuttered and he stepped out of her way.

She felt him watching her as she headed down the hall and found herself wondering what staying in his cabin would have been like. She concluded that being sequestered with him would probably be pretty grim. Abruptly, the unexpected protectiveness she'd seen in his eyes earlier played through her mind. Recalling the sense of security it had carried, she glanced over her shoulder.

Before his expression again became masked, she caught a flash of impatient anger... the kind a person experiences when an unwanted responsibility is suddenly thrust on them. Well, she hadn't asked for his help, and she had no intention of ever asking for it. Shoving the man out of her mind, she continued to the study, which her grandaunt had graciously given her to use for an office.

For the remainder of the afternoon, she wrote. By the time evening came, she was feeling much more optimistic.

"The letter was probably a one-time thing and is meaningless," she told her grandaunt at dinner that night.

"People shouldn't be allowed to write such things," Wanda declared. Then her face brightened. "I have something for you." She nodded toward a small box sitting near Gillian's plate.

Picking it up, Gillian was aware of a muted cheerful sound like wind chimes in the distance. Inside, she discovered an oblong crystal approximately an inch and a half in length, wrapped in gold wiring and suspended on a gold chain.

"You hear them, too, don't you?"

Gillian looked across the table to see her grandaunt watching her with a gleam in those old eyes. For a moment she considered denying it. She didn't want people looking at her askew the way they did her grandaunt. But she couldn't lie to Wanda. "Yes, I do. When I was young, I used to think you had a music-only radio station you listened to once in a while. Then one day I was standing by the window in front of them. I heard soft music playing very faintly. Then Bobby Kyle from up the street came along. I had a crush on him, but as he passed, suddenly the music I was hearing became an unpleasant discord. I looked down at your crystals and realized that was where the sound had come from. Clearly they were not as enamored with Bobby Kyle as I was."

Wanda frowned thoughtfully. "The crystals don't mind Bobby." The twinkle returned to her eyes. "Maybe they were just warning you that he wasn't the right man for you."

"Maybe," Gillian replied. Gingerly, she picked up the necklace. Her touch caused it to chime softly. *Be still,* she ordered silently and the chiming ceased. At least this one seemed to be cooperative, she thought gratefully.

"You listen to your crystal," Wanda ordered. "It will warn you of danger."

"I will," Gillian replied. She wasn't so certain she could really rely on the gemstone as the perfect watchdog, but in a way she didn't understand, she felt a certain comfort having it.

Chapter Two

Gillian stood looking at the envelope her grandaunt was extending toward her. Two days had passed since the first disturbing letter had arrived, and she had convinced herself that she would receive no others. Now she knew she'd been wrong. Even without opening the envelope, there was no doubt in her mind this letter was from the same lunatic. The way the address was printed was identical, and again there was no return address.

As she reached for the letter, her crystal issued a high-pitched note of distaste. She would rather burn the thing than touch it, she conceded silently. But destroying the letter would serve no useful purpose. Grasping the envelope by the corner so as not to disturb any fingerprints, she sliced it open. Carefully, she extracted the letter and read it. Her instincts had been right.

"I'll call Thatcher Brant," Wanda said, picking up the phone directory.

"Another fan letter?" a male voice asked.

Gillian turned to discover Taggart had joined them. He was frowning, and for the second time she had the strongest impression he didn't like being involved in her problem. "Yes, but it's nothing for you to concern yourself about."

The frown on his face deepened. "I don't want to see you hurt."

The thought that she would have enjoyed his protection if it wasn't being so grudgingly given played through her mind. Mentally, she scowled at herself. The man considered her a pain in the neck. "Now that I'm forewarned, I'm sure I can guard my back."

"It never hurts to have a second pair of eyes watching, as well."

Her gemstone was playing a long, low, mellow series of notes as if it found Taggart of particular interest. *Your taste in men leaves something to be desired,* she admonished it silently, and the music stopped.

"Thatcher will be right over."

Gillian jerked around to see her grandaunt hanging up the phone. For a moment Taggart had so claimed her attention she'd forgotten Wanda was still in the room. "There, you see, Mr. Devereux, I will have a second pair of eyes watching over me."

He nodded, turned and left.

Listening to his footsteps retreating down the hall, she congratulated herself for reading him correctly. He'd been looking for an escape, she'd given it to him, and he'd grabbed it and run.

"Men!" Gillian fumed under her breath a short while later. After giving the letter and envelope to the chief of police, she'd walked Thatcher to the front door.

Taggart had been standing on the porch casually leaning against one of the square white posts holding up the roof.

Thatcher stopped and offered his hand in greeting to the handyman. "I thought you were being kept pretty busy with orders for handcrafted furniture."

Accepting the handshake, Taggart shrugged. "Got tired of being up on my mountain. Thought I'd take a job in town for a few weeks. Wouldn't want people thinking I'm antisocial."

For a moment Thatcher regarded him narrowly, then he nodded. "As long as you're here, you could help me keep an eye on Gillian."

"Sure," Taggart replied.

"I wouldn't want to impose on Mr. Devereux, " Gillian spoke up quickly.

Thatcher turned to her. "There's no dishonor in accepting aid. Taggart's got a sharp eye. I'll feel better knowing he's keeping it on the lookout."

Gillian had forced herself to smile with acceptance, then she'd gone inside. A couple of steps down the hall, she'd stopped and was now fuming. Only a short while ago, she'd freed Taggart of any responsibility and now the chief had placed it squarely on his shoulders once again. She turned to go back outside and inform Taggart that he could disregard Thatcher's request when she realized the men were still talking.

"Is there anything I don't already know that I should be made aware of?" Thatcher asked.

"Nope," Taggart replied.

Gillian scowled. Did the chief think she'd left out some important detail? Men! she fumed again. They always trusted each other to know more than any female.

"I'll expect to hear from you if you do suddenly have any ideas on how to handle this situation," Thatcher said.

"I'll let you know," Taggart promised.

Her ire building, she waited in the hall until Thatcher had driven away. Then she started toward the door. She was in midstride when Taggart entered. Attempting to avoid a collision, she jerked her step back and lost her balance.

"Whoa!" Taggart growled, his hand fastening around her arm to keep her from falling.

Her near-clumsy landing on the floor was wiped from her mind by the steellike strength of his fingers. Her whole attention seemed to immediately focus on him and his touch. She was sure she'd never felt a hand so strong.

"You look like a woman in a hurry," he said, satisfying himself that she was steady, then releasing her.

Her freedom sent a sense of desertion sweeping through her. *This letter business has my mind behaving bizarrely,* she mocked herself. This man was not a willing ally. "I heard Chief Brant ask you to watch over me, and I wanted to assure you that was entirely unnecessary."

"I don't mind watching over you."

She was about to call him a liar, but the words died in her throat. An unexpected spark of masculine appreciation was glistening in the blue depths of his eyes. A heated glow began to warm within her. Then she saw a coldness descend over his features and realized he wasn't pleased that he'd exhibited even a momentary attraction.

Catching a glimpse of herself in the mirror, she frowned. "Just because I haven't spent a great deal of time preening myself doesn't mean you have to be embarrassed because you find me acceptably good-looking as I am."

He regarded her dryly. "I find you more than acceptably good-looking, and I'm not embarrassed to admit it."

"But I'm not your type," she finished for him.

"I just figure it's better if we keep our distance."

"No one can accuse you of not being blunt." Her gaze raked over him. "As long as we're being honest, you're not my type either."

He suddenly grinned. "Sounds as if we should get along just fine then."

"As long as you mind your business and let me mind mine," she replied. But as she turned and started down the hall to her left, she couldn't help thinking that he'd looked unexpectedly handsome when he smiled. Shrugging off the thought as inconsequential, she continued to her office.

A few minutes later she was scowling at her computer screen. She'd just described the hero of her book, but instead of his eyes being brown and his hair blond, the eyes were midnight blue and the hair black. Taggart was not her idea of a hero! she declared mentally, and quickly erased the screen.

The walls of the room began to feel as if they were closing in on her. Deciding she needed a break, she turned off the machine, found her grandaunt and informed her that she was going for a walk into town.

"Maybe you shouldn't go alone," Wanda said worriedly.

Gillian shook her head. "I will not allow a nut case to keep me prisoner. Besides, whoever is sending these letters is more than half a continent away."

"I suppose you're right," Wanda conceded.

Gillian gave her a reassuring hug. "I know I am." Then with a wave, she headed to the front door.

She'd gotten just beyond the white picket gate at the end of her grandaunt's walk when the sound of hurried footsteps behind her caught her attention.

"I'll walk along with you," Taggart said, joining her.

Again her crystal hummed a musing tune and again she hushed it. "I'm sure I can find my way on my own."

"I'm sure you can. But I need a couple of things from the hardware store. So, either I follow ten paces behind or walk with you."

"You're a stubborn man, Taggart Devereux," she growled, coming to a halt and frowning at him.

A sudden mischievous gleam sparked in his eyes. "I've been called worse."

She couldn't stop herself from grinning back. "I'll bet you have."

Abruptly his expression again became businesslike. "So do I walk with you or follow behind?"

Either way his presence would make her uncomfortable, but the set of his jaw told her his mind could not be changed. "Suit yourself," she replied over her shoulder, already again heading toward Main Street.

He fell into step beside her. "Never liked looking like a parade."

Trying not to be so aware of his company, Gillian glanced across the street. Penelope O'Malley was weeding her garden. Gillian had noticed that whenever anything was going on in the neighborhood, this gray-haired, willow-thin widow with a hawkish nose seemed to be busy in her garden. Further proof no stranger could come down their street unnoticed, she mused. "Penelope's front garden gets well tended. I wonder how her back garden fares." A flush suddenly tinted her cheeks when she realized she'd spoken aloud.

"About as well as her front," Taggart replied. "She likes to keep an eye on everyone around her. How do you think Wilber Delany's grandchildren found out about him comforting Sarah Childs after she was widowed last winter?"

Gillian recalled how the elderly couple had been amazed that anyone had known about their seeing each other. They lived next door and had used their back doors when visiting. Gillian frowned thoughtfully. "She must use binoculars. The Delany and Childs's houses are nearly half a block away."

"Where there's a will, there's a way."

A way to discourage him from insisting on accompanying her occurred to Gillian. "Aren't you worried she might start a rumor about us?"

"Makes no difference to me. And from what I've seen, you're not dating anyone, either."

She shrugged a confirmation.

"A romance author with no real romance in her life."

A taunting edge in his voice rankled her. "I simply haven't met anyone who could hold my interest."

"Maybe your fantasies have made it impossible for a flesh-and-blood man to compete."

She glanced toward him to see a cynical expression on his face. "I never write about perfect men. Everyone has their faults. That's what makes us human." Deciding that turnabout was fair play, she added, "What about you? Since you seem to think I need an excuse for not being attached, what's yours?"

"Never found anyone who'd put up with me."

"I don't buy that. I've noticed several of the single women in town coming up to flirt with you after church."

He cocked an eyebrow as if to imply he was surprised she'd noticed.

Well, maybe she had been paying more attention to him than she'd even realized. He did seem to stand out in a crowd. However, she wasn't ready to admit he'd caught her attention a few times. "I'm a people watcher. I get a lot of material for my books that way."

Unexpectedly, he grinned. "Those women are just interested in my body."

Gillian grinned back dryly. Her gaze raking over him, she intended to remark about him having a surprising sense of humor, but the words died in her throat. He was a hunk.

"I was sure you'd have a snide comeback for that one," he said, when she remained silent.

Get a grip, she ordered herself. His body might be appealing, but she refused to give the appearance of drooling. "I didn't want to bruise your male ego," she tossed back.

"Truth is, women never leave well enough alone. They're always wanting to change things...furniture...life-styles...their husband's habits. I'm pretty set in my ways. I like both my house and my life the way they are."

"Compromise is part of any lasting relationship."

"I guess I've just never met a woman I've been willing to compromise to please."

She noted the hard set of his jaw and recalled his insistence on accompanying her. "Or maybe you're just too stubborn to consider bending even a little."

"Maybe," he conceded.

Startled by his honesty, she could think of nothing to say and the remainder of their walk into town was done in silence.

Reaching Main Street, Taggart refused to run his errands and meet her on the town square. Instead, he insisted they remain together. Realizing that arguing would be useless, she grudgingly conceded to his wishes.

It was not an uninteresting experience, she found herself admitting, upon her return home. They'd caused several heads to turn, and she'd actually seen two of the more elderly townsfolk begin talking behind their hands. She'd written about that in books but had never actually seen it done before. "This has been an enlightening experience," she informed Taggart as they stepped up onto the porch. "From now on when I write about my heroine being the object of town gossip, I won't have to use my imagination."

"Noting who's pairing with who is an important pastime in small towns," he returned. "But don't worry about our names being linked for too long. Someone's bound to say something to me, and I'll set the record straight."

Gillian frowned. "There's nothing I'd like better than to have the record set straight, but I don't want people knowing about the letters. It's embarrassing."

"I'll tell them you're writing about a man who does carpentry and painting for a living and were accompanying me to get a more complete picture of the occupation."

"Good heavens," Wanda exclaimed, meeting them as they came through the front door. "I just got off the phone with Penelope O'Malley. She wanted to know how serious the two of you were about each other. I told her it was a shame a young couple couldn't walk down the street together without tongues starting to wag." She suddenly smiled. "But you do make a good-looking pair."

"Looks aren't everything," Gillian said, passing her grandaunt and continuing to the kitchen to put away the groceries she'd purchased.

"We'd mix about as well as oil and water," Taggart added, following with the bag he'd insisted on carrying.

"Vinegar and oil," Wanda corrected, entering the kitchen as Taggart set his bag on the counter. Her grin widened. "A very spicy combination." Her gaze raked across both of them. "It wouldn't hurt for either of you to settle down. Taggart, you could use a couple of heirs and, Gillian, you've always said you wanted children."

Gillian frowned. "I've never thought of you as being so ardent a matchmaker."

"It was the crystals that put the idea into my head. They suddenly started playing the wedding march when you two came walking up the street. Somehow it felt right."

Taggart left the room, shaking his head.

"Sounds more like wishful thinking on your part," Gillian said over her shoulder while putting the milk in the refrigerator.

"Well, I would feel more comfortable if you were married and had a strong man looking after you," Wanda conceded.

"I have two strong men looking after me," Gillian pointed out.

"I suppose." Wanda frowned. "But it's not the same as having a husband. Maybe you spend too much time writing those books and not enough time living."

Gillian started to protest but stopped. "These past couple of years I have been sort of hiding away from the world," she admitted. "But even when I was dating, I couldn't find any man I wanted to tie myself to."

"I certainly hope you don't intend to stop trying," Wanda admonished. "My Bill had his faults, but he made life interesting. I miss his companionship."

Gillian frowned thoughtfully. "I would like a man in my life. But he's going to have to be a lot more flexible than Taggart Devereux."

"I suppose Taggart is a bit set in his ways," Wanda conceded.

"He's as set as the cornerstone of a skyscraper," Gillian declared.

Wanda abruptly grinned. "However, there are other fish in the sea. I'll keep my eye out for possible prospects."

Mentally Gillian groaned. She was not in the mood for her grandaunt to do any matchmaking. "I'll keep *my* eye out," she said, her tone letting her grandaunt know that she wanted to choose her own mate.

Wanda merely smiled more broadly. "It can't hurt for both of us to take a long look around."

Gillian shook her head as she walked down the hall to the study. This morning she only had a lunatic fan to worry about. Now she had a matchmaking grandaunt. "Where did I go wrong?" she muttered under her breath.

"What's happened now?"

She'd been staring at the floor while she walked. Looking up, she saw Taggart. He'd been spreading tarps in preparation of painting the hall. Now he was watching her with an impatient scowl. "Grandaunt Wanda has decided to play matchmaker. She thinks it's time I had a husband."

His scowl darkened.

Gillian gave him a dry look. "Don't worry, you aren't a candidate."

His expression remained grim. "Seems to me this isn't the best time for Wanda to be inviting a parade of men into the house. I know the locals by sight, but if she starts bringing in visiting grandsons and nephews from out of town, I won't know if it's your 'fan' coming in the door or one of her possible matches."

Again his grudging protectionism irked her. "Maybe you and I'll both get lucky and she'll find someone who appeals to me. Then I'll have a husband to watch over me, and you can go back to minding your own business with a clear conscience."

He continued to scowl. "Yeah, maybe," he muttered, returning to spreading the tarp.

Her hands rested on her hips and she glared at him. "You don't have to make it sound as if you think my finding a husband is such an impossible task."

He straightened to his full height. "Truth is, I read one of your books last night. I doubt any man could live up to your expectations."

"You're wrong." An impish gleam entered her eyes. "In fact, twenty years ago, you'd have made the perfect hero...stoic, grim, arrogant beyond belief, authoritarian, always right and master of all he surveyed, including the heroine."

"I'd never claim to be master of all I surveyed and most certainly not of any female." Turning away from her, he again applied himself to spreading the tarp.

Taggart Devereux was a royal pain in the neck, Gillian thought, continuing into the study. She sat down at her computer, and this time had no trouble recalling that her hero had blond hair and brown eyes.

Chapter Three

Gillian stood looking down at the handful of mail she'd brought in from her grandaunt's mailbox. Along with grocery fliers and sweepstakes entries, she could see the corner of a white envelope and knew another "fan" letter had arrived. After the second one, they'd begun arriving daily.

But now it was not the contents of the letters that had her shaken. Pulling out the envelope, she looked at the postmark. This one had been mailed from Philadelphia, Pennsylvania. The second had come from Las Vegas, the third from Denver, the fourth from St. Louis and the fifth from Chicago. Now her fan was in Philadelphia.

"I don't like this. He's getting closer."

Gillian looked up to see Taggart peering over her shoulder. "I'm not ecstatic about it, either."

Even knowing it most probably didn't matter, she still handled the letter carefully as she extracted it from the envelope. The contents were the same as the others—

paragraphs from her books interspersed with long, rambling messages about how the two of them were soulmates and belonged together. She was certain there would be no fingerprints on the letter other than her own and those of anyone who handled it after she did. The envelope, on the other hand, would be covered with partial and blurred prints from its handling by the postal system.

Thatcher was keeping a file of the fingerprints found on the envelope. He'd even had the local postal people come in for fingerprint matches so that he could eliminate theirs. But she doubted his collection of prints would be useful. And, she knew he did, too. A state forensic expert had examined the stamps for possible saliva residue to be used in the event they came up with a suspect, only to discover tap water had been used to wet the glue. Whoever her fan was, he was meticulous about not leaving any evidence that could lead to him.

Her crystal began to issue an unpleasant note of discord. She'd grown used to it reacting to her moods and told it to hush. It hit a sour note as if it was angry with being ignored, then fell silent. A crystal with an attitude, she groaned. What next?

The ringing of the doorbell caused her to jump. "I hate the way these letters have made me feel afraid," she seethed, putting down the letter and heading to the hall.

To air the paint fumes from the house, the windows and back door had been left open, along with the wooden front door. Through the screen door, Gillian recognized the tall, handsome, blond-haired man and pretty, chestnut-haired woman on the porch. When it rains, it pours, she thought ruefully, then admonished herself for being unkind. Their insistence, in addition to a grudging gratitude and a lingering sense of duty to her deceased friend,

Ida, had forced her to keep in fairly close contact with this pair. They were, in fact, some of the very few people who knew exactly where to find her. But she would have preferred that they were at home in California and not standing on her doorstep at this moment.

A shrill note rang out from her crystal. *All right, all right, so I owe you an apology. You were trying to warn me,* she soothed it silently. *Consider me warned. Now be quiet.*

Forcing a bright smile, she opened the door and stepped aside to allow the pair to enter. "Harold. Evelyn. What a surprise."

"I was in Boston on business and Evelyn came out to join me. We couldn't leave the East Coast without seeing you." Harold wrapped his arms around her and gave her a hug.

"You're looking tanned and fit," she said, admitting to herself that he was certainly one of the handsomest men she'd ever known.

As soon as Harold released her, Evelyn stepped up and took his place. Having hugged Gillian, she stood back, her hands still on Gillian's shoulder. "Well, you certainly have let yourself go. You look absolutely dowdy," she announced with a disapproving frown.

Evelyn had always been painfully honest, Gillian recalled. "I prefer to think of it as my healthy, earthy look."

A speculative glimmer entered Evelyn's eyes. "It looks more like a hiding-out look to me. I can't believe you let that creep who killed Ida do this to you."

The woman had always been perceptive, too, Gillian added.

Harold scowled reprimandingly at Evelyn, then smiled warmly at Gillian. "You look wonderful to me."

Apology showed on Evelyn's face, and she gave Gillian a second hug. "I'm sorry. I've always been too blunt for my own good. California has been lonely without you."

Gillian grabbed the opportunity to turn the conversation away from herself. "It can't be that lonely. You're looking as lovely as ever." This was no lie. Gillian knew the woman had turned thirty-five her last birthday, but Evelyn didn't look a day over twenty-two, and her classically beautiful face did not have a single wrinkle. "I'm sure you still have your bevy of men hanging around, or have you finally settled on one in particular?"

Releasing her and stepping back, Evelyn laughed, raked a hand through her long, thick tresses and cast Harold a sideways glance. "I haven't found anyone as mature or dependable as my brother yet." Her gaze traveled beyond Gillian and a speculative gleam entered her eyes. "But I'm always on the lookout."

Gillian heard footsteps approaching from behind. She'd been aware that, like a protective shadow, Taggart had been lingering near the living room entrance. Now, taking Evelyn's flirtatious remark as a cue, he was joining them.

Politeness forced her to introduce him. "Evelyn and Harold Hyatt, this is Taggart Devereux."

Evelyn's smile warmed even more. "Now I understand why Gillian has stayed here all this time. Maybe I should try the earthy look."

"It's always a pleasure to meet a friend of Gillian's." Harold held out his hand to Taggart.

Gillian saw the cord in Harold's neck twitch ever so slightly and knew his smile was only a mask. Ida had been the one to point the twitch out to her. "Whenever my husband doesn't like something or someone, he has this little tick in his neck," Ida had told her, and after that, it had become a compulsion with the two of them to always turn to Harold and watch his neck whenever he was being introduced to a new person, new food or new situation. Then they would glance at each other and the urge to laugh would build. Once they'd actually had to leave the room as the pain of holding in their giggles caused tears to form in their eyes.

Evelyn placed an arm around Gillian's shoulders, bringing Gillian's mind back to the present. "I hope you're treating our Gillian well." Her tone made it clear she thought Taggart and Gillian were romantically involved.

Gillian started to correct her, but Taggart spoke first. "I'm just here painting the house, and I'd better be getting back to work." With a nod of goodbye, he turned and walked away.

Evelyn's attention remained on his departing back. "If I could find a painter like that I'd have my place redone at least twice a year."

She reminded Gillian of a cat ready to pounce. Taggart's a big boy, he can take care of himself, she told herself. Still, a nudge of irritation toward the chestnut-haired beauty stirred within her.

"Hello," Wanda called out, coming from down the hall from the direction of the kitchen. "I was out back weeding my garden." She squinted for a better view as her gaze traveled over the newcomers.

"This is Harold Hyatt and his sister Evelyn, Grandaunt Wanda," Gillian informed her.

Recognition showed on Wanda's face. "You're Ida's husband and sister-in-law." Sympathy replaced her curiosity, and she took Harold's hand in both of hers. "I'm so sorry about your wife. I wish I could have met her. I know Gillian thought very highly of her."

Harold smiled warmly. "Thank you. We all did."

"She was a darling," Evelyn affirmed.

Wanda motioned toward a nearby doorway. "Go along into the living room and make yourselves comfortable. I'll make some coffee or tea, whichever you prefer."

Evelyn needed no encouragement. "Sounds lovely," she said over her shoulder, already on her way. "Harold hates to stop. We drove nearly all the way from Boston with only one quick break. I'd love some tea. Herbal if you have it."

"I've got some wonderful chamomile," Wanda called after her.

"We really didn't come to be a bother," Harold apologized, offering Wanda his arm.

"It's no problem. I love meeting Gillian's friends," she assured him. "You'll just have to excuse me for moving so slowly."

"I'll run ahead and turn on the water for tea," Gillian offered, gladly willing to allow her grandaunt to entertain the Hyatts. But as she started past the entrance to the living room, she realized she'd made a serious error.

"Gillian! When did this arrive?" Evelyn demanded, waving the fan letter in the air, then striding back into the hall on an intercept course.

Harold turned ashen. "What?" Releasing Wanda, he reached his sister in two long strides and grabbed the letter from her.

"I wish you hadn't touched that." Silently, Gillian berated herself for not remembering she'd left the letter open. "Chief Brant likes to have as few people handle them as possible."

Evelyn frowned, her gaze boring into Gillian. "Them? You've had more than one? From the same person?"

Wanda looked to her grandniece. "If that one came today, then it makes six."

"I can't believe this is happening again," Harold muttered.

Gillian saw the horror in his eyes. The letter was similar to the ones Ida had received, and she knew he was remembering his wife's death. "Really, I'm sure it's nothing to worry about," she assured him. "The police have the situation under control."

"They know who's sending these, and they're watching the man?" he demanded.

"Not exactly. But if any stranger shows up in town, everyone will be watching him. They do that anyway in small towns. People here protect their own."

"Chief Brant has Taggart keeping an eye on Gillian, as well," Wanda interjected. She scowled at the letter. "People who write things like that should be locked up."

Evelyn nodded. "I couldn't agree with you more."

"I don't like this." Harold took Gillian's hands in his. "We knew who was writing those letters to Ida, and the police still couldn't keep him from killing her. I won't stand by and allow the same thing to happen to you."

"Really, I feel quite safe," she lied.

"When we get to the Wainwright Inn, I intend to make my reservation for an indefinite length of time. I'm not leaving town until I'm assured that you are out of danger," he declared.

"I'm staying, too," Evelyn added.

Inwardly Gillian groaned. Outwardly, she forced a smile. "You're overreacting. Really, we have everything under control here. Now, let's have that tea. You can tell me what our friends back in California are doing."

For a moment Harold looked as if he was going to pursue the subject of her fan, then, abruptly, he smiled patronizingly. "Yes, of course. Let's talk about more pleasant subjects for a while."

That was another thing that had always irritated her, Gillian thought, continuing into the kitchen to turn on the water. Harold treated women as if they were children who needed to be coddled. However, as long as he was willing to drop the subject of the letters, she was happy.

Two hours later, standing on the porch waving good-bye to the Hyatts, Gillian wanted to scream. She'd tried to discourage them from staying but had been unsuccessful.

"I figured you'd try to jump at the chance to have me replaced as your protector."

Gillian turned to see Taggart joining her. "Having you trailing around after me is bad enough," she replied. "Having Harold and Evelyn would be impossible."

"My crystals didn't like that pair," Wanda said from the rocking chair into which she'd sunk to wave her goodbye to their guests. "They were constantly chiming off-key."

Gillian had noticed. However, not wanting to give Taggart something to ridicule her about, she did not give a verbal confirmation but simply nodded in acknowledgment of her grandaunt's statement. She knew he'd think she was merely placating the elderly woman. "Harold and Evelyn were very good to me after I was hit by the car. Harold visited me every day in the hospital and saw that I always had fresh flowers. And Evelyn came regularly, too, with all sorts of games and hobbies to keep me occupied. But they can be overbearing. They made me feel smothered."

"They're very alike," Wanda mused. "Not that they look so much alike, although there is a family resemblance, especially around the eyes. But they have a lot of the same mannerisms and I noticed they finished each others' thoughts several times."

"Their parents are divorced. The mother has been married several times since, and the father, as well. From what Ida told me, Harold and Evelyn were constantly being shifted back and forth between them, neither parent being interested in keeping the children permanently. I heard Evelyn once joke that she'd felt like a hot potato people were always trying to get rid of. I think the two of them formed their own private, stable family unit and looked to that for security. On top of that, they're twins and, from all I've heard, in many cases twins have closer bonds than other siblings."

Wanda nodded. "I've seen that happen."

Hoping to relieve some of the tension the Hyatts' visit had caused, Gillian gave her shoulders a shake. "They both adored Ida, and they've been extraordinarily kind to me. I feel guilty about not liking them more."

"Some chemistries just don't mesh," Taggart said, breaking his silence.

Gillian's gaze swung to him. His expression was unreadable but she couldn't stop herself from thinking that his remark was directed at her and him as much as it was toward her feelings for the Hyatts. "Maybe that's nature's way of keeping people from making destructive alliances."

"Then either nature doesn't do such a good job or a lot of people don't pay any heed to their instincts," Wanda interjected.

"It's my guess the latter is what happens," Taggart said. "Sometimes temptations can be too great even when we know they're only going to get us into trouble."

His gaze had locked onto Gillian's as he spoke. In the blue depths of his eyes, she saw a heat that caused her knees to threaten to buckle. "But how can you be so sure the temptation will only lead to disaster?" she heard herself arguing.

"There are some cases when a person just knows." Abruptly he straightened from his leaning position against the wall. "I've got to get back to work."

Gillian watched the screen door swing closed behind him. The attraction she'd seen in his eyes was genuine. But then so was the rejection. Furious with herself for having given even a hint that she might be interested in him, she scowled. "That has got to be the most inflexible man I've ever met. If he searched the entire universe, he probably couldn't find a wife who'd put up with him."

Wanda frowned thoughtfully. "He can be hardheaded, but he's dependable and honest and goodhearted. Always has been, even as a youngster."

"It's hard to picture him ever being a child."

"I have to admit, he always was a mite on the serious side. I remember when Wendel Chamers drowned in that fishing accident...must have been twenty years ago now. Wendel was nearly eighty and had lived a good long life, but Taggart took the death real hard. I never really understood why, either. 'Twasn't as if he was close to Wendel or even Helen, Wendel's wife. They were just folks he knew. Course Helen had been his Sunday school teacher for a number of years. Anyway, for the first few months after the funeral, he went by the Chamers house every day after school to run errands and do odd jobs for her...as prompt as clockwork. And he refused any pay. After a while his visits became less frequent, but up until the day she died, he'd drop in on her at least once a week to offer his services."

"He does seem to be intractable when he takes on a cause," Gillian muttered. "I wouldn't mind his appointing himself my guardian if I thought he really cared about me, but I hate the idea of being a duty that he was unlucky enough to be assigned."

"Well, I, for one, am greatly relieved to know you have him looking after you," Wanda declared.

Gillian sighed deeply. After the Hyatts had left, she'd tried to work but, before leaving, they'd insisted she join them for dinner. The thought of a long, boring evening ahead had nagged at her the rest of the afternoon. Now it was nearly time for them to pick her up, and she was contemplating pleading a headache. That, however, would be unkind. After giving herself a final once-over in her bedroom mirror, she headed to the living room to say goodbye to her grandaunt.

Taggart was sanding the woodwork in the hall. Wanda had invited him to stay for dinner so she wouldn't have to eat alone, and he'd accepted.

Glancing over his shoulder at her approach, a cynical expression came over his face. "For someone who claims to want to get rid of a man, you look more like the flame attracting the moth."

Gillian couldn't deny she'd taken pains with her appearance. She'd swept her hair up into a sophisticated style, applied just the right amount of makeup to enhance her features but still keep a natural look, and she'd chosen her red suit to wear. The skirt was straight, hemmed just above the knees. The jacket had a feminine cut, tucking in at the waist to show off the curves of her figure.

"You do look fetching," Wanda said as Gillian continued on into the living room.

She saw the concern in her grandaunt's eyes. "Don't worry. I haven't changed my mind about getting rid of Harold." Gillian grinned mischievously. "This is my 'taking care of business' look."

"It resembles the Gillian I remember a lot more than the one who's been playing the wallflower since she arrived in town," a male voice said.

Gillian glanced over her shoulder to see that Taggart had joined them. His expression was shuttered and she wasn't certain if he approved or disapproved. "I want to assure Harold that I don't need him here to protect me."

His gaze raked over her for a second time. An exaggerated leer in his eyes mocked her. "If you were trying to get rid of me, that suit wouldn't work."

"If there is a way I could get rid of you, I wish you'd tell me," she returned dryly.

"Gillian!" Wanda frowned at her niece, then turned to Taggart to include him in her gaze. "I wish the two of you would settle on a truce. You set my crystals to chiming so loudly, I can barely hear myself think."

For a long moment, a silence filled the room. It was Taggart who broke it. "Sure, I'll agree to a truce," he said. Reaching Gillian in three long strides, his hands closed around her upper arms.

Startled, she stood dumbly, uncertain of what to expect. Then his mouth found hers. She'd written about kisses that awoke a desire so intense the heroine felt as if a fire had been ignited within her, but she'd never experienced one until now. Pride told her to push away, but her body refused to obey. It wanted this to last forever.

Suddenly she was being released. Her hand clutched a nearby chair to steady herself.

"When I was a kid we sealed our truces by spitting on our hands and shaking. Figured you'd prefer a different method," he said blandly, as if this not only explained but excused his behavior.

The heat of his lips continued to linger. "A simple handshake would have sufficed," she replied stiffly.

"Truces should never be taken lightly. They have to be sealed properly."

Again she was certain she saw a flash of heat in his eyes, then in its place was ice. Clearly he was attracted to her but, equally clearly, he'd found something about her he didn't like and refused to allow himself any warm feelings toward her. Well, she had her faults, she admitted, but none were that serious. If either of them had a real problem, it was him. He was obviously not only hardheaded but narrow-minded. Pride brought the strength back into her legs. "Next time, I suggest we bury a hatchet."

Her tone intimated she had already chosen the bull's-eye and he was it. He grinned wryly. "I'll remember to keep my distance in the future."

"Children!"

Both turned to see Wanda shaking her head.

Taggart's manner became businesslike. "I've got some woodwork I need to finish sanding." His gaze leveled on Gillian. "If your dinner engagement doesn't go well, I want you to call here. I'll come pick you up. I don't want you out after dark alone."

"I'll call a taxi."

"Bruce Wiley runs the only taxi service in town, and he closes down his business at nine unless you've made special arrangements before then," Wanda interjected.

There were a few inconveniences to living in a small town, Gillian conceded. Ire sparked in her eyes. One of them was having to put up with the likes of Taggart Devereux. "I'm sure I can find my way home just fine."

"That last letter came from Philadelphia. That's too close for me. I want your word that you'll call Taggart," Wanda insisted.

Gillian saw the fear building in her grandaunt's face. She didn't like upsetting the elderly woman. "All right. I promise, I'll call Taggart if I need a ride home."

Wanda sighed with relief while Taggart nodded his approval, then strode out of the room.

Her capitulation had left a bitter taste in Gillian's mouth. Taggart was the last person in the world she wanted to turn to for help. Vowing she would find an alternative if the need arose, she bid her grandaunt goodnight and went out onto the porch to await the Hyatts' arrival.

But it wasn't the Hyatts who arrived. It was only Harold.

"Evelyn was still dressing when I left," he explained as he drew near. "I thought we'd have dinner at the inn. I understand it's the best place in town."

"I believe it is." Not wanting another encounter with Taggart, she added, "Shall we go? I'm starved."

Harold smiled and offered her his arm. "I like a woman with a good appetite."

She caught the double entendre in his words and cringed. He was flirting with her. She hadn't expected that. Maybe Taggart had been right about this suit.

"I'm glad we have these few minutes alone," he said, opening the passenger door for her.

Uncertain of how to respond, she merely smiled back. As he rounded the car, she noted that he looked like a man with purpose, and her muscles tensed. She didn't like the way this evening was beginning. Maybe she was reading him wrong, she told herself hopefully.

Harold climbed in behind the wheel, but after inserting the key in the ignition, he paused and took her hand. "You've been on my mind a great deal during the past couple of years, Gillian. A great deal."

"I really appreciate all you and Evelyn did for me while I was in the hospital," she replied, politely attempting to work free from his hold.

He gave her hand a final squeeze, then released her. "Helping you through those difficult days kept me sane. I was devastated by the loss of Ida."

Gillian recalled his drawn and ashen countenance. Tears for her departed friend burned at the back of her eyes, and a surge of sympathy for the grieving husband swept through her. "We all were."

"I loved my wife dearly," he continued, starting the car and pulling out onto the street. "And I knew how close she was to you. That was the reason I first began coming to visit you. I knew Ida would have wanted me by your side, seeing you through the ordeal of your recovery."

Gillian's uneasiness grew stronger. During the past months she'd noticed that the frequency of his letters and phone calls had increased. She'd reasoned that he was still having trouble getting over Ida's death and was looking to her for comfort. Now she began to suspect she'd been very wrong in that assumption.

He pulled over to the curb and turned off the engine. Giving her his full attention, he again took her hand in his. "It was during those times when I'd help you with your therapy or we'd simply sit and talk that I began to develop more tender feelings for you. My first reaction was guilt. Ida had barely been gone. I told myself that it was your sweetness and your close friendship with my wife that caused you to have a special place in my heart."

"And I'm sure that is the case," Gillian insisted. "You were so desperately in love with Ida. You couldn't possibly have truly cared for me. What you were feeling was something similar to a rebound reaction."

His hold on her hand tightened possessively. "I tried telling myself that, as well. When you left California I was relieved. But the relief lasted only a short while. I worried about you. I thought about you constantly. It was Evelyn who made me face my real feelings. I care deeply for you, Gillian."

"I will always think of you as a friend." She emphasized the word *friend,* hoping he would get the message.

He smiled self-consciously. "I'm coming on too strong. I know this is a shock to you. I'd planned on simply spending some time with you this trip, beginning my courtship slowly. Then I'd come back again next month and the month after."

Gillian felt her stomach churning. The last thing she wanted was to be courted by Harold Hyatt. "I care for you, Harold, but as a friend." She knew she was dealing a low blow, but she was desperate. "I will always think of you as Ida's husband."

His expression became stern. "I've had to face the fact that she's gone, and it's time you did, too. As I was saying, I wanted to go about this slowly. But discovering you've been receiving letters from a lunatic makes that impossible. I can't simply bide my time."

"This is all too sudden for me," Gillian hedged, frantically searching for a way to get out of this situation without hurting his feelings.

An expression of understanding spread over his face. "It's my timing. These letters must have evoked painful memories for you. Ida must be very strong in your mind right now."

"She is," Gillian replied, honestly.

He stroked her cheek gently. "I shouldn't have put any added pressure on you at this time. You already have enough. I should have been more patient. I'll try. I'll be your friend for now."

Gillian forced a smile of gratitude.

"And now, as a loving friend, I will see that you are fed properly." Putting action to his words, he started the motor and pulled back onto the street.

The guilt Gillian had felt during those times when Harold had visited her in the hospital came back sharply. He'd been very good to her. Still, as hard as she'd tried, she'd never really been able to make herself truly like him.

Mentally she breathed a sigh of relief at the sight of the Wainwright Inn. Evelyn waved from a rocking chair on the porch, and Gillian found herself actually glad to see the woman.

During dinner she tried to convince the two of them that she was perfectly safe without their continued presence. But neither of them would budge. Both declared they would stay and see her through this ordeal.

It took all her effort to keep a smile on her face while they drove her home. As they turned onto Peach Street she was a little surprised not to see Taggart's truck parked in front of her grandaunt's house. Apparently he'd changed his mind about waiting around in case she needed a ride home. And good riddance, she declared, glad she wouldn't have to face him again tonight. Also, to her relief the house was dark except for a light in the hall and the front porch light. "I'd ask you in, but it looks as if my grandaunt has retired for the night and I don't want to disturb her."

"Yes, of course," Evelyn replied. "To tell the truth, I'm exhausted. This has been a very distressing day."

Gillian agreed. Again thanking them for the dinner, she hurried to make her escape.

"I'll see you to your door," Harold insisted, already out of the car before Gillian could protest.

The way he placed his hand on the small of her back caused a curl of irritation. She recalled how he used to walk with Ida that way. The thought of a puppet master guiding his toy popped into her mind. She had to get away from him as quickly as possible. If she didn't, her polite facade might crumble. By the time they reached her door, she had her key in hand.

"I'll be by tomorrow. We'll go somewhere for lunch," he said.

She forced apology into her voice. "I've really got to work. I'm on a deadline."

"All work and no play makes Gillian a dull girl," he warned. He combed a strand of hair back behind her ear. "I'll be by to see you."

Before she could offer another protest, he was on his way back to the car. Reaching up, she flicked her hair out from behind her ear. "My cup runneth over," she muttered as she entered the house and locked the door. "A pervert and Harold Hyatt. Not to mention Taggart Devereux."

"I don't think I like being lumped in with those other two."

Gillian gasped and jerked around to discover Taggart standing near the entrance to the living room. "What are you doing here?" she demanded. "I didn't see your truck out front."

"I pulled it around to the back. I said I'd be here if you needed a ride home."

She frowned at the darkened room behind him. "You were just sitting there in the dark waiting for the phone to ring?"

He leaned against the wall in a nonchalant fashion. "I wasn't feeling much like explaining my presence to strangers. Figured if the lights were off, your friends would realize your grandaunt had retired for the night and maybe be polite enough not to disturb her."

Tired and in no mood to exchange barbs with Taggart, Gillian motioned toward the door. "Well, now that I'm home, you can be on your way."

"Afraid not." He straightened. "After you left, Wanda and I decided it'd be safer if I stayed here while I was finishing up this job. She seemed to feel more comfortable with the idea of having a man around, especially at night."

Gillian stared at him dumbfounded. "You're serious? You're actually going to bunk down here?"

"I'll be on the couch." He nodded toward the interior of the living room. "In fact, I was just about to doze off when you came home."

Gillian looked more sharply at him and for the first time realized he was standing in stockinged feet and wearing only a T-shirt with his jeans. "That couch can't be comfortable to sleep on."

"I've bedded down on worse."

"I really think you're carrying your word to look after me a bit too far."

"My word is my bond." He frowned. "A person could break into this house, there could even be a loud struggle, and Wanda would sleep through it. Without her hearing aids she's deaf as a doornail."

Gillian hated to be beholden to the man, but he did have a point. Besides, the set of his jaw let her know his mind was made up. "Suit yourself. Good night, Mr. Devereux."

"Night," he returned, heading back into the living room. Silently he cursed himself as he stretched out on the couch. He couldn't allow his emotions to become involved where Gillian was concerned.

A cynical smile tilted one corner of his mouth. He'd slipped this evening. She'd looked too damn kissable to resist. But it had been a real mistake giving in to that impulse in front of Wanda. He'd spent most of the evening convincing her he hadn't meant anything by it.

And just now when Harold had walked Gillian to the door, it had taken all of his control to remain in the shadows and not make his presence known in order to interrupt any good-night kiss the man might have been considering. The scowl on his face deepened. Keeping his mind strictly on business wasn't going to be easy, but it was absolutely necessary.

Gillian smiled as she walked down the hall. Sleeping on that couch should cure him of wanting to stay here. But, even before she reached her bedroom, guilt began to nag at her. By morning he was bound to have a neck cramp or a backache. And it was because of her he was staying.

Changing destinations, she entered the study. Before her uncle's death, this room had been his domain. After his death, her grandaunt had added a few feminine touches. One of those included an antique walnut daybed inherited from Wanda's mother. Gillian had napped on it several times and knew it was comfortable.

Standing there staring at the daybed, she knew what she was going to do. She wasn't happy with herself. She would be encouraging him to stay. Then she thought of her grandaunt. If her "fan" did break in, there was a possibility Wanda could get hurt. Grudgingly, she admitted that having a man around the house wasn't such a bad idea. She just wished it wasn't Taggart. But it was and, as irritating as he was, he didn't deserve to suffer.

Going to her bedroom, she gathered up her nightgown, robe, slippers and clothes for the next day. Next she stripped the sheets off the bed and put on fresh ones. Then, returning to the living room, she knocked lightly on the wall at the entrance to announce her presence.

"What is it now?" Taggart growled, easing himself into a sitting position.

"There is no reason for you to sleep in here." Seeing him rubbing his neck, she added, "That couch is obviously uncomfortable."

"If you've come to offer me the daybed in the study, forget it. Wanda already did. It isn't any longer than this couch." He lay back down, propping his neck on one arm and his ankles on the other.

"I'm giving you my bed. The daybed fits me just fine," she said stiffly.

He continued to lie there. "I didn't come here to tread on your turf."

Gillian frowned at him. "You're difficult enough to get along with when you aren't grouchy. If you sleep on that couch and get a backache or a cramp in your neck, you'll be impossible."

"Go to bed, Gillian," he ordered.

She scowled at his prone body. "I'm going to sleep on the daybed. You can sleep wherever you please, and if you wake up with a stiff neck it'll be your own fault."

She was stripping out of her suit a few minutes later when she heard him pad down the hall past the study and into the bedroom next door. Her back muscles relaxed and she realized she'd truly been worried about him. Shaking her head at herself, she pulled on her nightgown and crawled into bed.

Chapter Four

Gillian awoke in a cold sweat. She'd been dreaming about the day of Ida's death. The remembered impact as the car careened into them had jolted her awake. She raked her hands though her damp hair. Panic mingled with terror was causing her to gasp for air. She forced herself to stop and take several deep breaths before she hyperventilated.

Glancing at the clock on the wall, she saw that it was just a little past two. She wanted to go back to sleep, but when she closed her eyes, her inner vision was filled with the last glimpse she'd had of Ida. Her friend's face, classically beautiful and usually perfectly made-up, had been a blur of blood mingled with strands of long blond hair across features frozen in a startled expression.

From across the room she heard a sound resembling wind chimes being blown wildly around by a strong wind. Recalling that she'd left her crystal on the desk, and realizing it was reacting to her fright, she ordered it to be still. The chiming ceased.

"I might as well work," she muttered, turning to the one escape that allowed her to relax after one of these nightmares.

She pulled on her robe, slipped her feet into her slippers and headed to the kitchen to brew a pot of coffee. The water had just started dripping through the grounds when she heard what sounded like several sets of wind chimes playing discordantly. In the next instant, Taggart came through the kitchen door. His hair was rumpled and the belt was missing from his jeans, evidence that he pulled them on quickly. His shirt was also missing and his feet were bare. Gillian didn't think she'd ever seen so impressive an expanse of chest in the flesh. Mentally frowning at herself, she pushed this thought out of her mind.

"Do you always get up this early?" he growled sleepily.

"I couldn't sleep so I thought I'd work," she replied, adding stiffly, "Sorry I disturbed you."

He rubbed the sleep out of his eyes, then peered at her more closely. "You look shaken."

"I had a bad dream." Still feeling wobbly, she sat down at the table to wait for the coffee to brew. "Seeing Harold and Evelyn again brought back a lot of memories I'd been keeping buried."

"Want to talk about them?" he offered, seating himself across from her.

Normally Taggart Devereux would have been the last person in the world she'd have chosen to confide in, but at the moment she felt the need to talk to someone, and he was the only one available. "I was recalling the day Ida was murdered. We'd met for lunch. She'd had a lot on her mind and we'd talked for a couple of hours. She wasn't able to resolve her problem and I didn't feel totally comfortable advising her. It was a personal thing. In the end, she decided that she was too upset about the obscene letters she'd been getting to make any decisions. She thought they could be causing her to think unclearly."

"Decisions made under stress are not always wise ones," Taggart noted.

"You're right," Gillian conceded, surprised by how natural talking to him felt. Talking to anyone at the moment would be soothing, she reasoned. Her friend's laughing face filled her inner vision and her mind returned to the elegant little tearoom where she and Ida had shared their final lunch. "'You know what I always say at times like this,' Ida said to me. I grinned and replied, 'Let's go shopping.' That was her cure-all for the blues."

Gillian fought back tears. "She'd just bought a skin-tight red dress she thought made her look exceptionally dangerous and she was right. Of course, she had the figure that could pull it off. We were laughing as we crossed the street. Then suddenly there was this car bearing down on us. It hit before we had a chance to react. I remember being airborne, then landing hard. She was lying on the ground maybe a foot away." Again she recalled Ida's bloodied features and those lifeless eyes seeming to stare at her in shocked surprise. Giving her shoulders a shake, she shoved the image back into the dark recesses from which it had come.

Wanting to think about anything but that day, her gaze swung to the coffeemaker. "Coffee's ready."

"Can I assume you'll be working in the study?" Taggart asked, breaking his silence. Obviously realizing he'd issued this more as a command than a question, he added stiffly, "I'll sleep better knowing you're right next door."

"I'll work in the study." She pushed back her chair and rose. Earlier today his attempt to control any of her actions would have rankled her. Tonight it didn't. "I know you're not happy about feeling responsible for my safety. And I'm not happy about having someone baby-sitting me. But, at the moment anyway, I'm grateful for your presence," she admitted.

He merely nodded, rose and headed out of the room. At the kitchen door, he paused and turned back to her. "I'm sorry about your friend. But you're going to be all right, Gillian. What happened to her won't happen to you."

Looking at him, his bulk nearly filling the doorway, she did feel safe. "Thanks. Even if you can't guarantee that, I needed to hear it."

Again he merely nodded, then left.

She poured the pot of coffee into a thermos and carried it along with her mug to the study. Seated in front of her computer, she'd just turned it on when a soft knock sounded, followed by her door being opened. It was Taggart.

"I'd prefer if you'd leave your door ajar," he said. It was more of an order than a request.

A part of her rebelled at relying on him so closely for her protection. But her nightmare continued to haunt her. "If it'll make you more comfortable, it makes no difference to me if it's opened or closed."

"Good, we'll leave it open."

As he started back to his room, Gillian frowned at the empty doorway. She hated being so scared that she could actually find comfort in Taggart Devereux's company.

Suddenly he was back at the entrance to her room. "I honestly don't mind watching over you," he said gruffly.

Before she could respond, he was gone. Sitting motionless, she heard the slight squeak of springs as he lay down on his bed. She didn't believe him for a second. That he'd actually tried to make a difficult situation easier for her surprised her. "He's a very confusing man," she murmured.

The memory of his kiss taunted her. She frowned at herself. She was certain of one thing. He was determined not to become romantically involved with her. And she certainly didn't want to become romantically involved with him. He was much too dictatorial and bull-headed.

Retrieving her current work from the hard disk, she allowed herself to become absorbed in the story she was telling.

Gillian awoke to discover her door closed and sunlight streaming in her window. Working had relaxed her, and around four she'd gone back to bed and fallen immediately to sleep. This time there had been no bad dreams. Glancing at the clock, she saw that it was mid-morning.

She owed Taggart. This was the first time since the letters had begun to arrive that she'd gotten some real rest. After dressing, she carried her coffee mug and the thermos to the kitchen. Through the window she saw Helen Ashbey from next door and her grandaunt. The women were sitting in the shade of the old oak in the big white wooden lawn chairs her grandfather had built, gossiping happily. "Just like a Norman Rockwell painting," she mused with a quiet smile.

Her crystal suddenly hit a discordant note. She scowled down at it. "What's wrong with you? I was actually enjoying a peaceful moment. I should have left you in your box."

The crystal hummed once again, then fell silent.

"Now don't go getting your feelings hurt." Realizing she was talking to an inanimate object, she groaned. She was beginning to behave like her grandaunt. Then she shrugged. "Some people used to have pet rocks. I have a pet crystal."

"You're up."

Taggart's curt tones caused her to jump slightly. Her crystal played a single note of the same discord, and she realized it had been his mood the gem had been reacting to. "And a good morning to you too," she returned dryly.

He drew a harsh breath. "Sorry. I was out back getting some supplies out of my truck. When I came in and discovered your room was empty, I wondered where you were."

His expression was again stoic, but she was certain she'd seen panic there when he'd first arrived. Guilt assailed her. "Look, Taggart, I want you to understand that if anything does happen to me, it won't be your fault."

"Just don't go anywhere without telling me."

His persistence was resurrecting her fear. Irritated to have her sense of safety so quickly destroyed, she tossed him a haughty glance. "Is it all right if I get something to eat?"

His gaze bored into her. "I want your word you'll tell me if you plan to leave the house."

She hated the thought of not being able to walk out into the sunlight unescorted, but she could tell that arguing would be useless. The man did seem to have a one-track mind and right now it was directed at guarding her.

"I'll let you know," she agreed grudgingly over her shoulder, heading for the refrigerator.

Standing with her back to him, pretending to concentrate on the array of food in front of her, she could feel him watching her and suspected that he did not entirely trust her. Then abruptly the prickling sensation ceased, and she glanced around to discover he was gone.

Taking out an apple, she bit into it while walking back to her office. Taggart, she noticed, was painting in the hall. From his vantage point she couldn't go anywhere without his noticing.

Sitting down at her computer, she stared at the blank screen. Fear again threatened to envelop her. It would be easy to stay in this house under his protective eye, she admitted. Immediately, self-directed anger swept through her. She would not allow a lunatic with a pen to imprison her. She wouldn't make the same mistakes Ida had made.

Grabbing her purse and keys, she went out into the hall. "I'm going into Griswoldville to pick up my mail," she informed Taggart, continuing toward the front door as she spoke.

"Wait a minute," he yelled after her.

She didn't stop. She didn't even look back. "I'll be back in an hour or so."

He caught up with her as she started to step off the porch, his hand closing around her arm and bringing her to a halt. "I'm going with you."

Jerking free, she faced him squarely. "No, you aren't. Ever since Ida died, I've been hiding, afraid to really live my life. But it hasn't prevented some pervert from finding me. It's time I got on with living. This guy could simply be a letter writer. I won't let him cage me in, and I refuse to allow you to dog my steps. You have a job and

a life. I don't want this lunatic to rob you of the freedom
to pursue both."

"I appreciate how you feel. In fact, under other circumstances I'd encourage you to come out of the rabbit
hole you've been hiding in. But now isn't the time.
You've been singled out, and you need to play it safe until this guy is identified and stopped."

"Even if he is identified, he'll get a slap on the wrist at
most. And there is no guarantee he'll stop sending the
letters. Besides, there is no protection in numbers. Ida
allowed herself to be trapped in her house for a while.
When she couldn't bear being behind those walls any
longer, she went out but only when she was accompanied by someone. Her caution didn't save her and nearly
got me killed in the process." Gillian started to her car.

Taggart fell into step beside her. "I'm coming with
you."

She frowned up at him. "No, you aren't."

"Morning," a female voice called out.

Gillian looked toward the street to see Mary Valdez,
their mail carrier, coming. Concern showed on the
woman's youthful, tanned face as she approached. "If
Taggart's trying to keep you from going off alone, maybe
you'd better listen to him," Mary said, extending a
handful of mail to Gillian.

Gillian knew Thatcher had made the postal people
aware of her letters. He'd had to in order to get their fingerprints. On top of the stack Mary handed her was a
now-familiar white business-size envelope with Gillian's
address printed in neat, precise hand. "Thanks," she
said, her confidence waning.

"Take care," Mary replied, then walked on.

The caution she'd read on Mary's face caused Gillian
to look more closely at the letter. Her chin trembled. The

postmark was from Smytheshire. "He's here," she said barely above a whisper.

"We need to call Thatcher." With a wave of his arm, Taggart motioned for her to precede him to the house.

Thoroughly shaken, Gillian obeyed without protest. Inside, she opened the letter while Taggart phoned Thatcher. As she read the contents, her face paled.

"What's happened?" Taggart demanded, hanging up and turning to see her ashen complexion.

"He says he's watching me, and that if he can't have me, no one else will." She dropped the letter on the coffee table and rubbed her hands hard against her pant legs, trying to scrub off the uncomfortable sensation holding it had left.

Taggart leaned over where it lay and read it without touching it. "Sounds like a threat to me."

Gillian nodded. In the next instant she was on her feet. "I've got to get out of here." At nearly a jog she went down the hall and into her bedroom. There she pulled out a suitcase and began to throw clothes inside. She was aware Taggart had followed her, but she ignored him.

"And just where do you plan to go?" he asked.

"Anywhere," she tossed over her shoulder, continuing to pack.

"He'll follow you."

"I won't stay here and put my grandaunt in danger."

"I'm an old woman. I'd be in more danger dying of a heart attack worrying about where you were than getting hurt by some lunatic with a poison pen in his hand."

Gillian paused to look toward the door and saw Wanda entering the room.

"You're safer here with Thatcher, Taggart and the rest of the neighbors watching over you than you'd be anywhere else," Wanda argued. "Why, even a stray dog can't walk down the street without people knowing about it."

"Acting on impulse is more likely to get you hurt than taking your time and thinking the situation out," Taggart added.

A knock on the front door interrupted. Not wanting to argue further with Wanda or Taggart, Gillian brushed past them to answer the summons. As she suspected, it was Thatcher.

"I'm going to leave town," she told him when she opened the door to let him in.

"Her pen pal has made a threat of sorts," Taggart said in answer to the questioning look Thatcher cast his way. He nodded toward the living room. "The letter's on the coffee table."

"No sense in doing anything rash. We'll talk about this." Thatcher motioned for Gillian to precede him into the room.

"I think it would be best for all concerned if I left now," she insisted, as they gathered around the coffee table while the chief read the newest missive.

"You're not going traipsing off on your own," Wanda snapped. "I won't allow it."

"You can't run the rest of your life," Taggart argued. "Just a few minutes ago you were telling me you refused to allow this lunatic to bully you any longer."

Thatcher set aside the letter and regarded Gillian calmly. "Right now he's only watching you. That'll give us time to spot him. He'd probably enjoy seeing you bolt. It would give him a sense of power and encourage him. Your best bet is to remain calm. Go about your daily routine. Just keep an eye on your back." Regret entered his voice. "I'm sorry I can't do more right now. I've only got one full-time deputy, and I need him for other duties. And, since all that's happened so far is that you've received a few letters, I can't justify hiring a second full-time man simply to guard you.''

''Even in big cities, they don't do that under these circumstances,'' Gillian replied, letting him know she understood the financial restrictions placed on him.

His gaze shifted to Taggart. ''You'll keep watch over her?''

Taggart nodded. ''You can count on me.''

''Good. My deputy and I will patrol this area of town more often.'' Unexpectedly, he grinned. ''And I'll stop by Penelope O'Malley's and tell her to give me a call if she sees any strangers on your street. It's been my experience that nothing gets past that woman.''

Her panic subsided some, and Gillian had to admit that they could be right. ''I'll stay for now. But at the first sign my grandaunt could be in any danger, I'm leaving.''

Wanda gave Gillian's hand a squeeze. ''We'll see this through together.''

Thatcher dropped the letter into a plastic bag and the envelope into another. ''I'll be close by,'' he promised, then left.

Allowing the chief to show himself out, Taggart continued to regard Gillian grimly. ''I want your word you won't run without giving us some warning that you're going.''

Still not totally convinced that staying was the right thing to do, Gillian didn't want to face another round of arguments if she should decide to leave. ''I'm not making any promises.''

''Gillian,'' he growled impatiently.

Wanda made a shooing motion with her hands in his direction. ''Don't you have a hall to paint? I'd like a few words in private with my grandniece.''

For a moment he continued to study Gillian, his gaze boring into her as if he could will her to do his bidding.

Her chin firmed.

"I've never met a woman so obstinate," he growled, then strode out of the room.

Determined to make her grandaunt understand the seriousness of the situation, as soon as she and Wanda were alone, Gillian turned to the one source she knew her grandaunt heeded. "The crystals understand there could be real danger."

"They have been making quite a racket," Wanda conceded. "Tom sulked out of the room a while ago." She frowned worriedly in the direction the big yellow cat had gone. "I do hope he isn't considering running away from home."

"I doubt very much that he'd allow his temper to interfere with his creature comforts," Gillian soothed. "Most likely, he's curled up on the rocking chair in your bedroom taking a nap."

"Most likely," Wanda agreed with relief. She returned her gaze to her crystals. "I could have told them to hush, but I stopped silencing them ages ago. Some are very sensitive to being quieted." She rose from her chair and crossed to the table in front of the window. "Calm down, my lovelies," she soothed, covering the glittering array with the velvet cloth.

An expression of reminiscence came over her face as she returned to her chair. "I can't recall just why. It was a long time ago. They were all making the most grating sounds. Not like today. Today they're issuing their general alarm. But that day, they were simply displeased with me." Her brow knitted into lines of concentration. "Yes, I remember now why they were so upset. It was before Bill and I were married. We'd had a terrible fight and broken up, and Jeremy Blythe had come to call. Anyway, I told them to shut up and give me some peace. Several of them didn't sing for months afterward. Since then, I simply cover them when they're being loud or off-key. They don't seem to mind that."

Gillian's own crystal was chiming. Closing her hand around it in a soft caress, silently she gently asked it to hush. Now I'm not only talking to it but worried about hurting its feelings, she chided herself. Shoving the crystal from her mind. she concentrated on her grandaunt. "I'm afraid, but not so much for myself as for you. I couldn't live with myself if anything happened to you because of me."

Wanda smiled reassuringly. "Nothing is going to happen to me or to you as long as you stay put. I trust Taggart and Thatcher. And I trust Penelope to let us know if anyone who doesn't belong on this street sets foot on it."

"I don't know." Gillian knew if she ran she would make herself an open target. Still, she remained nervous about staying.

Wanda's jaw firmed. "Well, I do. I'd never have a moment's peace with you on the run. You're staying right here, or you'll be responsible for me keeling over from worry."

"Like I said before, I'll stay for now." Silently, however, Gillian vowed that should the letters become more threatening, she would leave immediately.

Wanda smiled triumphantly. "Good. How about some lunch?"

The sound of car doors slamming, along with her crystal resonating in a low note of discord, brought Gillian to her feet. Hurrying to the window, she saw Harold and Evelyn coming up the front walk.

"We've come to take you on a picnic," Evelyn announced cheerfully when Gillian stepped out onto the porch to meet them.

Gillian forced apology into her voice. "I really can't go. I've got to get some work done."

"We won't take no for an answer. I warned you yesterday that all work and no play was bad for the soul," Harold reprimanded with a patronizing air.

"She received another letter. It was postmarked from right here in Smytheshire," Wanda said sternly, coming to stand beside Gillian. "And Thatcher Brant, our chief of police, made her promise she would stay at home."

Inwardly, Gillian cringed. She hadn't wanted Evelyn and Harold to know about this last letter. Seeing the shocked concern on their faces, her continued hopes of convincing them to go home grew fainter. "Really, having the letter writer here in Smytheshire is probably for the best. He can't move around this town without being seen, and once I know who to look out for, I'll feel much safer than worrying about some unidentifiable phantom lurking in the shadows."

"I want you to come back to California with me." Harold's tone was an order rather than a request. "My house has the latest security devices. I can keep you safe there."

Just the thought of entering Harold's house caused Gillian to experience a flash of claustrophobia. "I will not allow myself to be locked up."

Harold looked taken aback. "I'm offering you sanctuary."

She drew a calming breath. She had been much too sharp in her response. "I know," she said in a more level tone. "My nerves are just on edge. I do appreciate your offer, but I want to stay here. I ran once. It didn't work. This is my home now. I don't want to run again."

Evelyn smiled. "Even though I wish you'd reconsider and come home with us, I'm proud of you."

"I can't say that I'm pleased with your decision, but I will accept it, at least for now," Harold said. "However, no matter what Chief Brant has made you promise, we can't allow Mrs. Wainwright's picnic to spoil. She packed enough to feed an army—fried chicken, coleslaw, biscuits, marmalade, apple pie, freshly made lemonade or, if you prefer, a very good wine, and who knows what else. So since you can't leave your home, we'll just have to have our picnic in your backyard." He turned a charming smile on Wanda. "And you must join us."

"We'll ask that intriguing-looking painter, as well," Evelyn insisted. "As long as I'm going to stay in town, I might as well occupy my time meeting new and interesting people."

The thought of watching Evelyn flirt with Taggart throughout an entire meal left a bitter taste in Gillian's mouth. She didn't care if the two of them got together, she simply didn't want to have to be a witness, she told herself. "I'm sure Taggart will be much too busy."

"He's here to work, not to socialize," Harold admonished his sister.

Clearly Harold was not pleased with his sister's choice of playmates, Gillian mused. But then he'd never approved of any of Evelyn's boyfriends.

"I have to eat sometime. And no one in their right mind would pass up Marigold Wainwright's cooking," Taggart said, suddenly behind them.

"Wonderful!" Evelyn chirped brightly. "You go wash up and we'll set the food out."

"Sorry about this invasion of your home," Gillian apologized to her grandaunt as Evelyn and Harold returned to their car to gather the food while Gillian and Wanda headed to the kitchen for additional utensils and plates.

"This is your home, as well," Wanda replied. "Besides, watching Evelyn try to snare Taggart could be entertaining."

Gillian had a sudden vision of Evelyn in Taggart's arms. The image disturbed her. It's nothing personal, she assured herself. She'd always disapproved of the way Evelyn strung men along and then dumped them on a whim. "For his sake, I hope he stays away from her."

"It's nice to know you're concerned about my welfare."

Startled to discover Taggart had joined them, Gillian glared at him. "I wish you'd quit sneaking up on me."

Ignoring her reprimand, he studied her from behind a shuttered mask. "I assure you, I'm always cautious where women are concerned."

Gillian had the distinct feeling he was referring more to her than Evelyn. "You have nothing to fear from me, Taggart Devereux," she assured him haughtily.

He shook his head. "Don't underestimate yourself, Gillian Hudson. I don't plan to." Turning to Wanda, he asked, "Could you use some help?"

"You can take this tablecloth out and spread it on the picnic table," she directed.

Gillian scowled at his departing back. Clearly he considered her nothing but trouble. Silently she wished Evelyn good luck. Taking Taggart down a notch or two would be good for the man. Almost immediately, she took back that wish. As much as he irritated her, she didn't want to see him get hurt.

"Watching you and Taggart spar has added spice to my life."

Gillian saw Wanda grinning. "I'm glad one of us is enjoying it," she returned curtly.

Wanda's expression became thoughtful. "I still think the two of you would make a good pair."

Gillian merely shook her head at her grandaunt's suggestion. But as she carried the extra place settings outside, she found herself recalling the heat of Taggart's lips. Then there was the way he'd looked last night . . . hastily pulled-on jeans, barefooted, his hair disheveled. A heat began to build within her. *I will not be attracted to a man who considers me a gigantic nuisance,* she fumed at herself, turning her attention to Evelyn and Harold, who were coming around the corner of the house.

An hour later Gillian was beginning to think this could possibly be the longest afternoon of her life. Evelyn had consumed a great deal of the wine and was flirting unabashedly with Taggart. Although Gillian found it difficult to read him clearly, he seemed to be enjoying the attention. He'd actually smiled a couple of times, which had only served to egg Evelyn on.

With the two of them occupying each other's attention, she and Wanda had been left with Harold's company. He'd spent the past half hour trying to convince her to come back to California with him. The desire to plead a sick headache was growing stronger with each passing moment.

"I hate to intrude," a female voice called out apologetically.

Gillian saw Penelope O'Malley coming around the corner of the house. Instantly she became alert. The fear she was holding under tight rein threatened to take over. Out of the corner of her eye, she saw Taggart start to rise.

Like a guard dog being called to duty, she thought. And, in spite of how much he irritated her, she felt safer.

"Don't worry, dear, I haven't seen any strangers," Penelope added hurriedly.

Gillian drew a relieved breath. Penelope was here, no doubt, to gather fodder for her gossip. However, Gillian was happy for any intrusion. "You're always welcome. Would you like something to eat? We have plenty."

"No, but thank you."

Penelope was within a few feet of them now, and Gillian could see the stricken expression on her face. There might not be a stranger on their street, but something had upset the elderly woman greatly. "What's wrong?"

"It's Tabatha. She got out of the house. I was wondering if she's here with Tom? Your doors have been open a great deal, with Taggart carrying equipment in and out all the time."

Gillian had only seen the large white-haired Persian from a distance. Never allowed outside, the cat's favorite perch was on the back of a sofa set in front of Penelope's living room window, from where she watched the world through the glass with as sharp an eye as did her mistress. "I'll look," Gillian replied, already on her way in search of Tom.

He was, as she'd suspected, curled up in the rocking chair in her grandaunt's bedroom.

"Oh, dear!" Penelope wailed. She'd followed Gillian inside and was staring down at Tom with tears brimming in her eyes. "Tabatha is an indoor cat. She'll never survive out on her own. That horrible dog of Vivian's will eat her alive."

Gillian had never seen Penelope so shaken. "We'll find her," she promised.

"I hate to ruin your afternoon," Penelope apologized again. "And I know you must think I'm a silly old lady, but Tabatha has been my companion ever since Frank died. I just don't know what I'd do without her company."

"I do understand," Gillian assured her. She was well aware that her grandaunt talked to Tom as if he were human. And she knew Wanda would be lost without her pet. Clearly the same was true of Penelope.

"Of course we understand," Harold seconded.

Gillian saw him behind Penelope. The patronizing edge in his voice grated on her nerves, and an amused glimmer in his eyes let her know he thought the elderly woman was slightly daft. But then that was the reaction she'd expected from him. He treated all women as if they were not entirely capable. "I'll look under the bed," she said, already getting to her knees.

The Persian wasn't there. While Penelope watched hopefully, Gillian began a thorough search of the room.

"Did you find her?" Taggart asked as Gillian finished checking the closet.

She turned to the door to see that the rest of the party had followed her inside, and they were now standing in the hall. "No."

Penelope looked even more as if she were going to cry.

"Don't worry, we'll find her," Taggart promised.

Gillian was surprised by the gentleness in his voice and the honest concern on his face. She'd expected him to be as cynical about Penelope's attachment to her pet as Harold had been.

"I'd be so grateful," Penelope choked out, a tear trickling down her cheek.

Gillian's attention returned to the elderly woman. "Of course we'll find her. Why don't you and Grandaunt

Wanda go back to your place and take another look around? Tabatha could have decided she's had her fill of freedom and gone home. Meanwhile, the rest of us will scour the neighborhood.''

Penelope gave Gillian's hand a squeeze, then looked to the others. ''Would you really?''

''Of course we will,'' Evelyn replied.

As the two older ladies headed across the street, Evelyn turned to Taggart. ''I had a much more interesting way in mind of working off that lunch than a cat hunt, but there's always tomorrow.''

He merely smiled down at her, then suggested they each go in separate directions so that they could cover a lot of ground as quickly as possible.

Gillian was searching the bushes on the north side of the Ashbey house when Evelyn's voice rang out.

''I've found her,'' the woman yelled as if she'd just spotted the chest of gold in a treasure hunt. ''Damn, she ran under Gillian's car!''

Evelyn was half under the car by the time Gillian, Taggart and Harold joined her.

''You've found her?'' Penelope called out with relief, rushing across the street with Wanda hobbling along behind.

''I'll have her in a minute,'' Evelyn promised, then let out a curse as the cat ran out from under the vehicle.

''Tabatha!'' Penelope shrieked.

As the cat dashed to her owner and allowed herself to be scooped up in loving arms, a police patrol car pulled up to the curb and Thatcher Brant climbed out. ''Is there a problem here?''

''Not now,'' Penelope replied. She smiled at the searchers. ''Thank you all so much.'' Then her attention returned to her pet. ''You scared me half to death,'' she scowled. Her nose crinkled with disgust. "And you need a bath. Where in the world have you been?" Already forgetting the others, she clucked at the feline with motherly indignation as she hurried on her way home.

"Penelope's cat got lost. We helped her find it," Taggart explained, his tone letting the chief know they had the situation well in hand.

Thatcher nodded.

"Nice to see you again, Chief," Harold said, before Gillian could introduce him. He nodded to his left. "This is my sister, Evelyn."

"Pleased to meet you, Miss Hyatt." Thatcher tipped his Stetson in Evelyn's direction.

She acknowledged him with a smile, then cast a mischievous grin in Gillian's direction. "You do grow them big and handsome up here in Massachusetts."

Ignoring her, Gillian regarded Thatcher in confusion. "You've met Harold?"

"I stopped by to see Chief Brant yesterday. I wanted to make certain that everything that could be done for your safety was being done," Harold explained.

Gillian cast Thatcher an apologetic glance, then leveled her gaze on Harold. "I have every confidence in Chief Brant."

"I know he'll do all he can," he replied.

She scowled at the lack of trust in Harold's voice.

He turned to Thatcher. "Sorry, Chief. I'm sure you'll take as good care of Gillian as your time and budget allow. But the police in California did all they could and that didn't save Ida."

"I don't plan to let what happened to your wife happen to Gillian," Thatcher returned in an easy drawl.

In spite of the chief's outward show of calm, Gillian sensed the tension rising between the two men.

"I have room for a piece of pie now," Evelyn announced, obviously realizing that her brother was getting on the policeman's nerves and deciding that a change of subject was in order. "Will you join us, Chief?"

"I need to be getting back on patrol." Thatcher touched his hand to the brim of his hat in a gesture of farewell, then headed back to the patrol car.

"I need to get back to work, too," Taggart said.

Evelyn's mouth formed a petulant pout. "I was hoping you'd join me for dessert."

The playfully seductive innuendo in her voice rankled Gillian. The woman was an open invitation. Again she told herself that Taggart was a big boy, he could take care of himself. Still, she found herself hoping he wouldn't accept.

"I try not to overindulge," he replied.

Evelyn's pout became even more exaggerated. "Too bad." She suddenly grinned and challenge flashed in her eyes. "Maybe I can convince you to reconsider. I'm going to be in Smytheshire for a while."

"Maybe," he conceded, then with a final nod of goodbye to the others, he went into the house.

His "maybe" caused an uneasiness in Gillian.

"It could take some time, but I will find the chink in that man's armor," Evelyn vowed.

"You've really got to stop trying to pick up strays," Harold admonished his sister as he and the ladies returned to the backyard.

"I've never thought of Taggart as a stray," Wanda remarked. "He's more the leader of the pack kind, although he does seem to enjoy traveling alone."

Evelyn grinned even more broadly. "I love lone wolves."

"You love wolves," Harold interjected disapprovingly.

"Taggart's no wolf," Wanda snapped.

Both of the Hyatts turned to her. "We didn't mean any harm," Evelyn apologized. "My brother just likes to pick on me, and I can't help egging him on. It's the devil in me."

"I'm sure Devereux is a fine man," Harold added.

"Yes, he is," Wanda confirmed. Disapproval of their teasing still evident on her face, she turned to Gillian. "I'm tired. I think I'll go in and rest a bit."

As Wanda disappeared into the house, Harold turned to Gillian. "I'm really sorry if we offended your grand-aunt."

"She's very fond of Taggart," Gillian replied, then heard herself adding, "He is dependable and takes his responsibilities very seriously." She was championing him! Well, he deserved it. He'd shown honest compassion for Penelope. Admittedly, that had surprised Gillian, considering that he treated her as if she were an albatross hung around his neck. Clearly it was their chemistries. They simply didn't mesh. Shoving thoughts of Taggart from her mind, she concentrated on getting rid of the Hyatts.

Evelyn was cutting the pie. "Can I cut either of you a piece?" she offered.

"None for me," Gillian replied.

Harold held up his hand. "Nor I."

Evelyn dropped a thick slab onto a plate. "I'll leave the rest for Taggart to remind him of me. You'll see that he gets it, won't you, Gillian?"

"Yes, of course." Gillian's nerves were at the breaking point. Instead of seating herself, she remained standing. "It was really sweet of the two of you to bring

all this, but I've got to get back to work. These letters
have thrown me off schedule, and I'm in danger of missing my deadline.''

Harold was frowning at Evelyn, clearly still disgusted
with her flagrant attempt to seduce Taggart. ''Maybe I
should get my sister out of here before she decides to try
to feed the pie to your painter while he's working.''

Evelyn's eyes glistened. ''What a wonderful idea.''

As she started to pick up the pie and head into the
house, Harold caught her by the arm. ''No, you don't.
You're going to eat your dessert while Gillian and I
straighten up, and then we're leaving.''

Evelyn turned to Gillian and grinned mischievously.
''He's always trying to protect me from myself.''

Gillian was certain Evelyn had had no intention of
taking the pie inside to Taggart. Her movement in that
direction had merely been to tweak her brother. And
Harold had risen to the bait.

Ida, Gillian recalled, had found watching the two of
them amusing. Her friend had also claimed to have gotten a great deal of material for her books from watching
Evelyn deal with men. Gillian, however, had never been
an admirer of anyone who used people, and Evelyn was
a user, especially where men were concerned.

While Evelyn ate her pie, watching the house like a cat
who knew her prey was inside, Gillian and Harold packed
up the picnic. He insisted on leaving the leftover food and
Gillian accepted without protest. All she wanted was to
get rid of the two of them as quickly as possible.

''You will remember to tell Taggart that I left that pie
for him,'' Evelyn instructed, as Gillian walked them to
their car.

''Yes, of course,'' Gillian replied, fighting to keep the
stiffness out of her voice.

Again Harold scowled at his sister. Then his expression warmed as he turned to Gillian. "Apologize again to your grandaunt for me. I'm really sorry we upset her."

"She'll get over it," Gillian assured him.

They had reached the car and were loading the picnic basket inside when Evelyn issued a curse under her breath. "I've lost an earring!" she fumed.

"I'll keep an eye out for it," Gillian promised, determined this development would not slow their departure.

"I can't leave without it," Evelyn insisted.

Harold closed the trunk and frowned at his sister.

She looked at him pleadingly. "These are my favorites. You gave them to me five Christmases ago."

"I suppose we could go back and check the grass around the picnic table," he conceded grudgingly.

As the three rounded the house, Gillian's crystal issued such a high-pitched note, Gillian winced in pain. *I'm trying to get rid of them,* she assured it. Praying the earring would be found quickly, she threw herself fully into the search.

Suddenly Evelyn straightened. "You two keep looking here. I've got an idea." Before either Harold or Gillian could respond, she was on her way to the front of the house.

This time, the note the crystal played sounded almost panicky. *It's beginning to be as afraid as I am that I'll never get rid of these two,* Gillian thought, certain Evelyn had come up with some excuse to seek out Taggart. She knew the woman could be persistent, but she'd never before seen her this adamant about conquering a man.

"What is she up to now?" Harold muttered, getting up and giving Gillian a hand to her feet.

They rounded the house to discover Evelyn half under Gillian's car.

"What are you doing down there?" Harold demanded.

"I remembered brushing my shoulder against my ear fairly hard when I was trying to grab that cat," she replied. She let out a cry of triumph. "And I was right. Here it is!"

Squirming out from under the car, she put the earring back on, then brushed herself off. "Darn, I've gotten grease on me," she complained. "I think I need a bath."

"Most definitely," Harold concurred.

Watching them pull away, Gillian breathed a sigh of relief.

Chapter Five

Thatcher Brant sat in a rocking chair on his front porch, his feet propped up on the porch railing and crossed at the ankles. To any passerby he looked like a man relaxed, enjoying a late lunch.

But Samantha knew her husband well. Just the fact that he was home at this time of day was enough to tell her something was on his mind. "Are you going to tell me what's bothering you or do I have to try to guess?" she asked, as soon as she'd gotten the baby settled down for an afternoon nap.

Thatcher looked at his wife. Her raven hair and gray eyes made him think of a gypsy. Or maybe it was that ancient crystal ball she'd inherited from her grandmother that put that image in his mind. "It's those letters Gillian Hudson has been receiving. The one that came today was postmarked here in Smytheshire."

Samantha experienced a rush of fear for Gillian. "Here?"

Thatcher nodded. "And Taggart Devereux's been hanging around Gillian for the past few days. He seems to have a knack for knowing where trouble will strike."

"His family is one of those who came when Smythe-shire was first founded. Like some of the rest of us, he could have a touch of Druid heritage in him," Samantha suggested.

"Maybe." Thatcher's expression grew grimmer. "Have you seen anything regarding Gillian in that crystal ball of yours?"

"I noticed it was glowing this morning and took a look. She was there with Taggart and a tall, pretty, chestnut-haired woman I didn't recognize. Taggart was in the middle."

"The other woman sounds like Evelyn Hyatt."

"And who is Evelyn Hyatt?"

"She's a friend of Gillian's from California. Her brother was married to the writer who got killed. From what I saw this afternoon, I'd say Miss Hyatt is making a play for Taggart."

"Sounds as if my crystal is seeing a romantic triangle."

Thatcher cocked an eyebrow skeptically. "Gillian and Taggart?"

"You and me?" she tossed back at him.

He grinned. "That crystal ball of yours does seem to spend a lot of time peering into people's hearts."

Before leaving the porch, Samantha placed a light kiss on her husband's lips. "Well, I hope Gillian wins. I think she and Taggart would make a great pair."

"I doubt they'd agree," he replied.

Gillian ripped a piece of plastic wrap from the roll and covered the remaining apple pie. She'd finished putting away the rest of the leftovers from the picnic, leaving the pie for last. Now she stood frowning at it. For the umpteenth time she told herself that Taggart could take care of himself. But then she doubted that, having lived in Smytheshire all of his life, Taggart had ever come across anyone quite like Evelyn.

"I should mind my own business," she told herself, and started to the study.

Taggart was painting at the far end of the hall. Instead of continuing on into the study, she paused to watch him. Evelyn would never have come to Smytheshire if it wasn't for her, Gillian reminded herself. She would feel responsible if Taggart got hurt and she hadn't warned him.

Taggart felt her gaze almost like a physical touch. It made him uneasy. This acute awareness of her threatened his guard. Setting the paint roller down in its tray, he turned to her. "Is there something you want to say to me?" he asked sharply.

Again he made her feel like an irritant. "No." Entering the study, she sent the door slamming shut behind her. "He can take care of himself," she seethed under her breath. But Evelyn's string of conquests insisted on playing through her mind. A minute later she was back in the hall. "Actually, yes, I do have something to say. Well, sort of..." She hesitated.

He'd returned to painting. Now he set the roller down once again. He had the distinct impression she was going to say something she knew he wouldn't like. He was trying to save her life. Why couldn't she cooperate? "I hope you aren't going to tell me you're thinking of going back to California with the Hyatts. You can be better protected here."

Just the thought of going anywhere with Evelyn and Harold sent a chill through her. "No, I'm definitely not going back to California with the Hyatts." She frowned. "But it is them I want to talk to you about. Actually, one of them. Evelyn."

He cocked an eyebrow questioningly.

"I just thought I should warn you. She has a low threshold for boredom, especially where men are concerned. She likes the challenge of the chase, but once she's captured her prey, the thrill is gone."

"I figured she was someone I'd be smart to steer clear of."

There! She'd warned him. Now her conscience was free. She told herself she could go back in the study and get to work. Instead, she heard herself adding, "She can be persistent."

He regarded her dryly. "It's been my experience that most women can be."

The hairs on the back of her neck bristled. He was mocking her. "I've seen her in action. I simply thought you should be warned," she said stiffly, then quickly returned to the study and closed the door.

She'd sat down at her desk and turned on her computer when a knock sounded, followed by Taggart's entrance. His expression was unreadable. "I didn't mean to make you angry. I appreciate your concern."

Embarrassment that she'd tried to interfere in his private love life had begun to torment her. "I don't want you getting the wrong impression and beginning to worry. I'm not planning to make a play for you. The only reason I spoke to you about Evelyn is because she's here because of me and I'd feel responsible if she played one of her little games with you."

A smile tilted one corner of his mouth. "I wouldn't want you to feel guilty about my heart being broken." His gaze softened and she felt herself being drawn into the warm blue depths of his eyes. Abruptly the smile vanished and his manner became cool. "I'll be certain to keep my guard up," he assured her in clipped tones, and strode out.

Gillian frowned as the door closed behind him. Again, for one brief moment, she'd sensed that he was attracted to her. Then, like before, he'd behaved as if those feelings were taboo. What had she ever done to him to cause him to be so determinedly cold to her? she wondered. She scowled at herself. Why should she care? If he was so small-minded that he'd determined to dislike her without even getting to know her, he wasn't worth giving a second's thought to.

Anger at herself for trying to protect him bubbled inside. Striding to her door, she flung it open and stepped out into the hall. "I promised Evelyn I'd tell you that she left the pie especially for you."

Surprise registered on his face.

"Just for my own edification, I'd really like to know what I've ever done to you," she blurted.

His surprise deepened. "You've never done anything. Our paths have almost never crossed before now."

"That's what I thought." Her anger deepened. "So you just arbitrarily decided to dislike me?"

His surprise was replaced by a shuttered mask. "I don't dislike you. I'm merely trying to get a job done here."

She couldn't believe she'd behaved so adolescently. Embarrassment caused her cheeks to flush scarlet. "I don't know why I brought this up. There's no reason for us to be friends. You're arrogant, stubborn..."

He cocked an eyebrow.

Her embarrassment multiplied. "There was no call for me to say that, either." She pointed to the study. "I'm going to go in there now and lock the door and stay there until my sanity returns."

Putting action to her words, she returned to the study. Seating herself at her desk, she dropped her face into her hands and groaned. She'd just made a complete fool of herself! Well, at least now he had a reason to dislike her.

Taggart frowned at the closed door. Gillian Hudson was proving to be much more of a problem than he'd anticipated. She was cute when she was mad and even cuter when she was frustrated. He'd had a strong urge to kiss the tip of her nose. He'd also had a strong urge to try to convince her that he wasn't as stubborn or arrogant as she made him out to be. He raked a hand agitatedly through his hair. It would not do for him to give in to those urges. Thank goodness she was safely locked in for a while. "Women," he muttered under his breath, and returned to his painting.

Gillian sat at the dinner table, unable to think of anything to say. For the remainder of the afternoon, she'd stayed in the study, thus managing to avoid Taggart. But sitting at the table with him was rekindling her embarrassment.

"You two are being especially quiet this evening," Wanda remarked.

"It's been a long day," Gillian replied, as if that explained her reticence.

Taggart nodded in agreement.

Wanda continued to regard them narrowly. "You two can be downright boring at times."

"I'll take that as a compliment," Gillian said. "There's been much too much excitement around here lately."

"Maybe you're right," Wanda conceded.

In spite of her declaration that she preferred silence at the moment, Taggart's continued reticence was beginning to grate on Gillian's nerves. She'd spent a great deal of time during the afternoon assuring herself she didn't care what the man thought of her, but still she found herself wondering if he was feeling insulted. Covertly, she studied him. He looked, she decided, indifferent. Clearly what she said, thought or did meant nothing to him. Willing herself to ignore him, she concentrated on her food.

"There's apple pie for dessert," Wanda announced, pushing back her chair and rising.

Gillian couldn't stop herself from glancing at Taggart.

"Well, no one in their right mind would let one of Marigold Wainwright's pies go to waste," Wanda spoke up, when they continued to remain silent. "I'm cutting us each a slice."

A knock sounded on the front door as Wanda rose to slice the pie. "I'll get it," Gillian volunteered, happy for any excuse to get away from the table. However, when she reached the hall, her steps faltered. Through the screened door, she saw the Hyatts.

"We thought we'd stop by and see how you were doing," Evelyn said, entering before Gillian even reached the door. She gave Gillian a bright smile. "I caught a glimpse of Taggart's truck still parked out back. Where is he?"

"Eating apple pie," Gillian replied, determined to be indifferent to the woman's pursuit of the painter.

"Really, Evelyn!" Harold admonished.

His sister merely shrugged a shoulder at him and continued down the hall toward Gillian. "And just where is he eating the apple pie?"

Gillian nodded in the direction of the kitchen. As the woman passed her, she forced a smile for Harold. "You and Evelyn might as well join us for coffee and dessert."

"I hope you don't mind us stopping by," he apologized. "I needed to see for myself that you were safe."

Gillian merely continued to smile and led the way into the kitchen.

Evelyn had slipped into the chair beside Taggart and was giving him her full attention. "I was hoping maybe you'd show me your place by moonlight," she coaxed. "Marigold Wainwright tells me you have a cabin on top of a mountain. I'd love to see it."

"Really, Evelyn, you could practice some subtlety," Harold reprimanded, taking the seat Gillian indicated.

"All right. I'll have some coffee and pie before Taggart and I leave," she replied.

Gillian was busying herself getting down extra cups, plates and utensils. Again she told herself that his love life was his business, but she couldn't resist watching out of the corner of her eye. He was smiling politely at Evelyn. "I'll be staying in town tonight," he told her.

"Then you can show me around your town. Give me a taste of what the locals do after dark," she purred.

"Taggart's staying here to keep an eye on Gillian," Wanda interjected primly. "He won't have time to be escorting anyone around town."

Gillian saw the displeasure in Harold's eyes.

"My, my," Evelyn mused speculatively. "And I could have sworn you and Gillian didn't get along well."

"Chief Brant asked me to help." A coolness in Taggart's voice made it clear there was no romantic involvement between himself and Gillian.

"If you'd rather go home, I'd be happy to spend the night," Harold volunteered.

Inwardly, Gillian groaned. After her encounter with Taggart this afternoon, she was certain he would grab this opportunity for his freedom.

"I gave the chief my word I'd see this through," Taggart replied in an easy drawl. "And I never go back on my word."

Gillian breathed a mental sigh of relief. In this instance she was glad he was a man of resolve.

Harold's gaze now swung to her. "Really, I would be more than happy to guard you. It would be an honor."

"I appreciate the offer, but it's not very practical. You can't remain here indefinitely. You have a business to run in California. Taggart is already here working on my grandaunt's house. Staying over simply eliminates a long drive for him."

"Lucky girl," Evelyn murmured.

A short while later, Gillian dried the last pan.

A smiled played at the corner of her mouth. Both her grandaunt and Taggart had managed, each in their own way, to get rid of the Hyatts diplomatically.

By the time Gillian had served the coffee, seated herself and taken her first bite of pie, Taggart had finished with his dessert. Pushing his chair away from the table, he'd excused himself, saying he wanted to finish putting a second coat of paint on the hall.

Taking her second bite, Gillian noticed her grandaunt eating much more diligently than usual.

Before the others were barely half-finished, Wanda was swallowing down her last morsel. She smiled apologetically at the other three. "This has been an exhausting day for a woman my age. If you don't mind, I'll just begin straightening up around you. I want to get to bed early."

Picking up her and Taggart's plates, she proceeded to the sink and began running dishwater.

Taking her cue, Gillian had lowered her voice and, leaning toward Harold but including Evelyn, said, "This whole business has been a strain on my grandaunt. I really should help her and then see that she gets to bed."

They'd both nodded sympathetically and quickly said their goodbyes.

At the door, Harold had asked if he could come by later when her grandaunt was settled, but again Gillian insisted she had to work on her book.

"And now that the kitchen is back in order, I'm going to make myself a cup of tea and go watch television," Wanda announced as Gillian put away the last pan.

Gillian frowned tiredly in the direction of the study. "I'm going to work some."

Taggart was in the hall putting away his equipment. At her approach, he glanced her way. "I've got all the fans going full speed. The paint fumes should be gone soon so you'll be able to sleep all right."

She could hear the motors running. Earlier that morning, he'd put a fan in a window in each room along the hall. During the afternoon, she'd noticed that the added ventilation had kept the air quality reasonably good. She nodded in acknowledgment of his words and continued into the study.

She'd just sat down to work, when he entered.

"I wanted to make sure your fan is set steady and won't fall," he said, continuing past her without a glance.

Still uneasy about her behavior that afternoon, she merely acknowledged his presence with a nod, then quickly returned her attention to her computer.

"The fan's fine."

"Thanks," she replied, keeping her gaze directed at the screen. Expecting him to leave, she was surprised when a pair of jean-clad legs remained visible out of the corner of her eye.

"From his clothes and the fact that his rental car is one of the most expensive luxury models, I'd guess Hyatt's a fairly successful businessman."

Stunned that he'd not only spoken to her but asked about Harold, Gillian looked up. As usual Taggart's expression was unreadable. "Very successful."

"He'd also be considered good-looking by most women I know."

"Women find him attractive," Gillian agreed.

"Wealthy, handsome, charming and attentive. In other words, a good catch." His tone suggested that he found her rejection of Harold puzzling.

"That depends on what a woman wants."

He cocked an eyebrow questioningly.

Leaning back in her chair, Gillian stared at the computer screen with unseeing eyes, her mind traveling back in time. "Ida and I first met in seventh grade and became fast friends. I think it was because all either of us ever wanted to do was to become a writer. When everyone else was discouraging us, we were each other's cheerleaders."

Gillian smiled softly at this memory, then the smile faded. "She met Harold when she was twenty. We were attending a community college during the day and waitressing at one of the more exclusive restaurants at night. After the first night she waited on him, he became a steady customer, always requesting one of her tables. His parents had a great deal of money. They'd set up him and Evelyn in business, and they were on their way to being wealthy in their own right. Evelyn, although you'd never guess it from the way she acts, has an extraordinarily brilliant analytical mind and is a whiz with computers. She designs software, and Harold markets it. But Ida didn't care about the wealth. Harold was, as you pointed out, charming and attentive. He swept her off her feet."

"But you weren't charmed by him?"

"At first I was. I thought Ida was one of the luckiest women in the world. Harold was seven years older than her and ready to settle down. When he asked her to marry him, I was happy for her." Gillian fell silent as remembered incidents caused her expression to darken.

"Your elation didn't last?"

Taggart's voice reminded her she wasn't alone. Why she was telling him all of this was a mystery to her. They weren't even friends. But then some things were easier to talk to strangers about, and she did feel the need to talk. "Fairly quickly I began to see a side of him I didn't like. He was manipulative, controlling. He wanted Ida's full attention and convinced her to quit school. She and I still met for lunch occasionally, but dinner or any activity scheduled after dark was forbidden unless it was at their place or unless he accompanied us. If he had to work in the evenings, he insisted she remain at home no matter how important the function was to her. He said he worried about her being out after dark."

Gillian glanced up at Taggart and grimaced self-consciously. "I suppose you think that maybe I was jealous. My best friend had found a new best friend, that sort of thing? Well, that thought occurred to me, too. But Ida confessed to me that he even resented the time she devoted to her writing. She only wrote when he wasn't at home.''

Gillian returned her gaze to the computer screen. "However, when her first book came out, he did throw one heck of a party for her. I believe he honestly loved her and was proud of her. He just found it difficult to share her with anyone. When she started getting the letters from her obsessed fan, Harold became even more possessive. He demanded that she quit writing. She tried to explain to him that her writing was her way of calming her nerves but he refused to understand. In the end, she wrote in secret to keep from upsetting him.''

Gillian sighed. "I know she loved him, but he was smothering her. She told me so that last day we went shopping. She'd threatened to leave him if he refused to understand that she needed some personal freedom." Her gaze shifted to Taggart. "I refuse to be under anyone's thumb.''

"You would prove to be a thorn," Taggart noted, then strode from the room. The thought of any man trying to keep her under his thumb brought a wry smile to his face. Admittedly, she'd spent the past couple of years cowering in fear, but he was seeing the real Gillian emerging, and she was one tough lady.

Gillian knew she deserved that jab after this afternoon. She also knew there was something she'd left unsaid that needed to be said. She found him in the kitchen getting a glass of water. "I figured you'd jump at the chance to free yourself of the responsibility you feel to look after me. I want to thank you for not turning it over to Harold." Having said her piece, she quickly left.

Taggart frowned. He'd had no choice. But even if he had, he'd never have turned her over to Harold. The man obviously liked to break women's spirits, make them dependent. Taggart didn't approve of that. He was also certain Gillian would have bolted in a New York minute.

Late into the night, Gillian lay in bed unable to sleep. Talking about Ida had brought back a multitude of memories and caused her to take a close look at herself. She'd allowed Ida's murder to send her into hiding, and now she was allowing this letter writer to curtail her activities even more. She'd told Taggart she would never live under anyone's thumb. But she was still allowing fear to hold her down.

Moreover, she was well aware that even if her "pen pal" was identified, there was little the law could do. If she continued to let fear rule her life, she would never again feel truly free. Vividly, she recalled how Ida had become a virtual prisoner in her own home and saw herself beginning to be ensnared in the same trap.

"I'm not Ida. And I've done enough hiding out," she declared. "No man is going to cage me."

Chapter Six

Shortly after ten the next morning, Gillian gathered up her purse and car keys, then went in search of her grand-aunt.

"I'm going into Griswoldville to pick up my mail," she informed her.

Wanda frowned worriedly. "Do you really think that's wise?"

"Yes," she replied firmly.

"Then I'll ride along with you. I want to do some shopping anyway."

Gillian recalled her last shopping trip with Ida and a wave of apprehension washed over her. "I want to go alone. Besides, isn't Helen coming by soon to take you to the quilting circle at church?"

"I can cancel. These old hands don't work as well as they used to. Mostly I just sit there and talk. It's Helen and the younger women who get the work done."

Gillian's jaw firmed. She didn't want to hurt Wanda's feelings, but she also didn't want to place her grandaunt in danger. "I need to go alone. I need to prove to myself that I'm still in control of my life."

Wanda didn't look happy but she nodded her understanding. However, when Gillian turned to go, she laid a restraining hand on her arm. "You've told Taggart that you're leaving the house, haven't you?"

Gillian had considered not informing him of her intent. But that, she conceded, was being cowardly. "I will."

"You will what?" Taggart's voice sounded from behind her.

She turned to face him. "I'm going to Griswoldville to pick up my mail. And I'm going alone. Yesterday I actually allowed myself to become a virtual prisoner in this house. But now I've come face-to-face with my fear and I'm ashamed of myself for giving in to it. I won't let this creep force me to live the way Ida did."

For a long moment he regarded her in silence, then said, "If you want to go to Griswoldville, go ahead. Just promise me you'll be careful and stay away from strangers."

"Of course I will." Stunned that he'd conceded to her wishes without an argument, she said a quick goodbye to her grandaunt and hurried out before he could change his mind.

On the porch, she paused to scan the yard, then up and down the block. The sun was shining, a warm breeze was stirring the leaves in the old oak in her grandaunt's front yard. Somewhere a bird was singing. Helen Ashbey was chatting with Penelope O'Malley in front of Penelope's. Both smiled and waved and Gillian waved back. No one could invent a more peaceful scene, she thought, continuing to her car.

Again the image of Ida lying on the street taunted her. That day had seemed cheerful, as well. Her crystal issued a note of discord and a curl of anxiety twisted through her. "I should have left you at home. You were a real nuisance yesterday," she fussed at it under her breath, and it fell silent.

The temptation to go back inside and lock herself in her room grew strong. Gillian's jaw tensed with resolve. She was not going to let fear rule her life!

Climbing into her car, she started the engine and began backing out of the driveway. At the curb she braked to look both ways before pulling out onto Peach Street. As she turned her head from one side to the other, she saw Taggart running toward her. There was fear on his face.

"Turn off the car and get out," he ordered, jerking open her door.

Without argument, she set the brake, turned off the ignition and climbed out. "What?" she asked shakily, looking around expecting to see a stranger lurking behind a tree or running down the street.

He pointed to a small pool of clear, oily liquid on the driveway. Approaching it, he squatted beside it and dipped his finger into it. "Looks like brake fluid."

Wanda had followed him out of the house, and Helen and Penelope were hurrying across the street.

"What's going on?" Helen asked.

"Looks like Gillian has a leak in her brake line," Taggart replied.

Penelope's eyes widened. "It's a good thing you saw it. Why, she could have been driving down one of our mountain roads when her brakes failed and gone right off the side.''

''Yes, she could have,'' Taggart agreed curtly.

''Oh, my,'' Wanda choked out.

Taggart's gaze leveled on Penelope and Helen. ''Have either of you seen anyone on this street who didn't belong?''

Helen paled. ''Are you suggesting this leak wasn't an accident? That someone might have caused it on purpose?''

''It's the pervert who's writing those letters, isn't it?'' Penelope demanded, her eyes even more rounded than before.

Gillian flushed. ''You know about the letters?''

Penelope gave her a patronizing look. ''I watch Oprah. And I saw Chief Brant leaving your house a while back with a couple of those clear plastic bags the police use to collect evidence. One looked like it had an envelope in it. Then he started making daily calls, increased the patrols down our street and asked us to keep an eye out for any strangers.'' Her expression became conspiratorial. ''I got suspicious and cornered Mary. She confessed you'd been getting some upsetting mail. I put it all together and it spelled *pervert* to me.'' Her gaze narrowed on Gillian. ''You're being stalked, aren't you?''

''I'm being harassed,'' Gillian admitted.

''Have you ladies seen any strangers?'' Taggart repeated, his impatience showing. The image of Gillian lying dead at the bottom of a ravine had him badly shaken. His instincts had barely warned him in time to save her. His jaw tensed with purpose. If that lunatic harmed one hair on her head, he'd pay dearly.

''No, no one,'' Helen replied, continuing to stare at the puddle as if it was a snake ready to strike.

Penelope shook her head. "Only Gillian's friends, and they aren't strangers to her." She smiled. "They're very nice young people. Would you thank them again for helping me find Tabatha?"

"Yes, of course," Gillian replied absently, concern for her grandaunt foremost in her mind.

"If I get my hands on whoever did this..." the elderly woman snarled.

"Maybe it was an accident. Cars do break down on their own," Helen suggested hopefully. "I just hate to think we have anyone lurking about who would do something so cruel."

"You're right, it could simply be a faulty line," Taggart conceded, but he didn't believe for a second that was the case. "I'd appreciate it if you ladies would go home now. I'll call Thatcher and have him come take a look before we disturb anything else."

Penelope nodded vigorously. "Clues. We don't want to disturb any clues."

Gillian noticed her grandaunt's hands trembling. Slipping an arm around Wanda's waist, she said, "Come on, we should go inside."

Without protest, Wanda allowed Gillian to help her into the house. In the living room, she sank into a chair. "I thought your crystal would be able to warn you of danger. But it seems they only react to people, not inanimate objects."

Gillian knelt beside the elderly woman. "I can't stay here. I don't think the leak was an accident. If I hadn't been so insistent about going alone, you would have been in that car with me. I won't put your life in jeopardy."

Wanda clutched her grandniece's hands in hers. "I don't want you to leave."

"I'm taking her to my place," Taggart stated, entering the room. "My dogs will sniff out any living thing that doesn't belong there." He turned to Gillian. "The chief will come by and take care of your car. You go pack."

Gillian's jaw firmed. "I won't put anyone else's life in danger."

He frowned impatiently. "You can't get away from people entirely. If you run, you could put some innocent bystander's life in danger. At least I'll know enough to look out for my backside."

The thought of him being injured because of her caused a hard knot in Gillian's stomach. "I'll find a place where I'll be alone. I have a friend who rented a cabin in the Rockies one summer. She said there was no one around for miles. I'll find a spot like that."

Taggart regarded her dryly. "I thought you told me you were finished with hiding out?" His expression became grim. "Besides, this guy is persistent. He'll find you again and then you'll be a sitting duck."

Wanda's hold on Gillian's hands tightened. "I never thought I'd hear myself saying this, but if you won't stay here, I want you to go to Taggart's place. It doesn't matter if the gossips' tongues wag. At least you'll be safe."

Gillian knew Taggart was right about her fan finding her. Still, she would not endanger him. "I'm not staying here, and I'm not going to Taggart's place. That's final."

Taggart's hand closed around her arm and he pulled her to her feet. "We need to talk . . . in private."

"There's nothing to talk about. You're not going to make me change my mind." Gillian attempted to pull free but he held fast.

"There's plenty to talk about," he growled. "Excuse us, Wanda."

Realizing fighting was useless, Gillian stopped resisting as he guided her down the hall and into the study. Once inside, he kicked the door closed with the heel of his boot, then released her. "If you leave, I'll have to follow."

She couldn't believe he was being so stubborn. "Don't be ridiculous. I'm absolving you of all responsibility for my welfare."

"You can't absolve me."

"Of course I can."

"I want your word that what I'm about to tell you will never leave this room."

Impatience flashed in her eyes. "There is nothing you can say that will change my mind. Now, would you please leave me alone? I have to pack."

As she started to move away, his hand again closed around her arm, forcing her to remain. "I want your word, Gillian," he demanded.

He was giving her no choice. "All right, you have my word. Just tell me whatever it is you have to tell me and then go away."

Releasing her, he took a step back. His expression was grim. "Sometimes I see things that are going to happen before they occur. Usually it involves someone dying."

Gillian stared at him dumbfounded. Taggart was the last person in the world she would ever expect to hear saying something like that. "You're claiming to be precognitive?"

"I'm not claiming it. I am," he growled, clearly displeased about having had to reveal this information.

"I don't believe it. You're too stoic, too both-feet-on-the-groundish, too good ol' boyish, too..." Realizing she was rambling, she clamped her mouth shut to stop herself.

"I didn't ask for this ability. It just happened. Seems my grandmother had it, too. According to her, there's Druid ancestry in our family."

"You're really serious about this," she murmured. Well, she and her grandaunt could hear crystals singing, she reminded herself. They even communicated with them. Her initial shock began to fade.

"It wasn't easy for me to accept at first," he continued curtly. "Wendel Chamers's death was the first one I saw. I didn't do anything about it. I thought it was just a nightmare. Then he died the way I dreamed it would happen."

Recalling what her grandaunt had told her, Gillian studied him narrowly. "So that's why you devoted yourself to taking care of his wife, Helen?"

He nodded. "My grandmother knew something was wrong. That's when she took me aside and told me about our ancestry. Seems there were Druids in our family lineage a few centuries ago. She blamed herself for not talking to me sooner. Of course, if she had tried to tell me before Wendel's death that I might have inherited this 'talent', I'd have thought she was daft. At first, I still didn't totally believe her. It occurred to me that my dream could have been a coincidence, and she was simply fitting fantasy to reality."

Gillian saw the self-consciousness on his face. His shoulders had straightened, and she knew he was bracing himself for a cynical response. But she wasn't feeling cynical. Instead, her every instinct was to believe in him. As proof she should follow those instincts, her crystal played a clear note of accord. "But something convinced you that your grandmother was telling the truth?'' she prodded.

He looked surprised that the skepticism had gone from her voice. Suddenly, understanding spread across his features. "You hear your grandaunt's crystals, don't you?"

"That's something I'd prefer we kept between us," she replied, realizing that what she'd thought was indulgent cynicism on his part toward her grandaunt was in reality unspoken acceptance of Wanda's claims. "What convinced you that your grandmother was not daft?" she asked, returning the conversation to him.

"The next time I dreamed about someone dying, it was Doc James. The doc fell asleep at the wheel, missed a curve in the road and went over a cliff. I couldn't ignore the possibility my grandmother might be right. But I figured if I went to him and told him about my dream, he'd think my ladder was missing the top rung or maybe even a few of the lower ones. So instead, I told him I was thinking of becoming a doctor and asked if I could hang around with him for a few days. He agreed."

Taggart's expression grew grim. "About four days later, Clementine Stuart called to say she was getting ready to deliver. She refused to go to the hospital. She was determined to have her baby at home. They live up on Hornet's Ridge. I recognized the curve from my nightmare when Doc and I drove past it on the way to the Stuart place. She was in labor nearly all night. In the end, she had twins, both healthy. When it was time to leave, I could see Doc was really tired. I was still too young to have my license, so I started talking a blue streak, hoping that would keep him awake. But it didn't work. When we neared the curve, I could see him beginning to nod off. As we started around the bend, his eyes closed. I grabbed the wheel. We nearly ended up in the ditch on the other side of the road, but we didn't plunge over the cliff. That fright kept him wide awake for the remainder of the drive to his place. We both figured it wouldn't be safe for him to drive me all the way home, though. My parents knew I was with him and weren't worried. So his wife put me in their guest room for the rest of the night. It was the first good night's sleep I'd had in a week. The nightmare was gone. The next morning I told him I'd changed my mind about being a doctor and went on my way. He's still alive and kicking today.''

Taggart frowned. "That experience taught me that I could change what was going to happen. But usually it's a one-time shot. And I've learned how to pinpoint the event fairly closely. But in your case..."

As his pause lengthened into a silence, Gillian's nerves tensed. "What about my case?''

"A couple of weeks ago, I had a vision of you lying on the floor in your grandaunt's living room. When the letters started arriving, I knew why you were dead, but I didn't see how your death had come about. And I still couldn't pinpoint the time. I just knew it would be soon. Then yesterday, when you went to get in your car, I suddenly had a flash of you going over a cliff. I knew that was going to happen within the hour if I didn't stop it.''

Gillian recalled the fear she'd seen on his face as he'd dashed across the yard. If she'd needed any further proof of his ability, she had it now.

"I'm not seeing you lying in your grandaunt's living room any longer, or at the base of the cliff,'' he continued. "But I'm still experiencing a strong uneasiness. I know the attempts on your life aren't over. I also know I'll see them before they occur, and I'll have to do something to try to prevent your death. So whether you go or stay, you've got me for a companion. I don't have a choice. But I do know I can protect both of us better at my place."

The full truth dawned on Gillian. "The reason you came looking for work here at my grandaunt's house was to watch over me."

"I'll arrange for someone else to finish the job. Right now I want you to pack." This was an order. Without waiting for a response, he strode out of the room.

Gillian stood frowning at the empty space he'd so recently occupied. His revelation explained a lot, such as why, although he obviously didn't relish the role of being her protector, he'd insisted on taking it on and had continued to accept the unwanted responsibility—even when presented with the opportunity to escape it.

Her pride rebelled at the thought of continuing to accept his help, but she knew he'd meant it when he said he would follow her if she left. Reasoning that he would be in less danger on his own turf, she went in search of her suitcase.

Gillian was not certain what to expect when they left the main road and started down a gravel lane bordered by woods on either side. There had been two mailboxes at the beginning of this private roadway. At about a quarter of a mile, the road forked. Taggart took the left branch.

She guessed his house would be a typical two-story frame dwelling, resembling other older farmhouses in the region. And being a bachelor who was more interested in his work than his accommodations, it would probably be in need of some repair. She visualized his workshop as a converted barn.

They'd come nearly a mile since the fork, all of it winding its way upward, and she was beginning to wonder just where he did live when they emerged into a large clearing. The house was nothing like she'd imagined. It was a well-maintained, sprawling, two-story log structure with a wide-roofed porch that wrapped around the sides and extended into a deck at the back. A little distance away was a long single-story, equally well-maintained frame building with two sets of extrawide double doors and several large windows to allow in plenty of sunlight. That, she concluded, had to be his workshop.

Two dogs, both of mixed breeds, one medium in size and shorthaired, the other huge and long-haired, came loping off the porch as Taggart parked his truck in front of the house. They stood barking loudly until he climbed out of the cab, then rushed to welcome him. His features relaxed and he smiled as he petted each roughly in greeting.

The honest pleasure and tenderness Gillian saw on his face shook her. Then the dogs spotted her. Both tails immediately stopped wagging and they stood, their bodies tense as if waiting for the merest incentive to attack.

"Relax, she's a friend," Taggart said.

Cautiously, they approached Gillian and sniffed her legs and feet. She was surprised the animals believed she was there by invitation. Taggart's voice had been polite but icy, and she noticed that his expression was again cool. Deciding she'd be safer if she reassured the beasts herself, she directed her full attention to them. "Hi, guys," she said, petting them, then scratching behind their ears. They responded by nuzzling her affectionately.

"The big one's Goliath and the littler one is Orion," Taggart informed her, retrieving her suitcases, then heading to the house.

When she started to follow, the dogs came along, flanking her on both sides. In spite of their seemingly friendly acceptance, she wasn't totally certain if they were honestly welcoming her or were acting as a guard detail, making sure she did no damage to their happy home.

At the door, Taggart leveled his gaze on the beasts. "Stay. Guard."

Immediately, like sentries, they lay down on either side at the top of the flight of steps leading up to the porch.

Taggart had opened the door, and now he stepped aside for Gillian to enter ahead of him.

The house was decidedly masculine in decor. A glimpse into the living room revealed brown leather upholstered furniture. The tables in there and in the hall were Early American in design and expertly crafted.

Leading her upstairs, Taggart came to a halt beside the second door to the left. "This will be your room."

Gillian followed him inside. The huge four-poster bed was the first thing that caught her attention. A bough of oak had been carved into the headboard. The top drawer of the dresser also had the same oak design while the rest of the furniture was free from ornamentation. "Lovely" came to mind but that didn't seem to be the proper word to use in this house. "It's impressive," she said instead.

"Thanks," came his reply as he set her suitcases on the floor.

Glancing toward him, she saw the pride in his eyes and a thought struck her. "You made these things?"

"I made all the furniture in this house. It's what I do."

"I'd heard you were talented. I just never realized how much."

"I'm glad you're impressed."

There was a gleam of pleasure in his eyes and she realized he did honestly care that she liked his work. Finding herself wanting to encourage this bud of friendship, she smiled back crookedly. "I am."

His gaze warmed. Then abruptly the polite coolness she was so used to again descended over his features. Turning away from her, he opened the bottom drawer of the dresser and began taking out sheets and pillowcases. "If I'd known I was going to have company, I'd have had Peggy make the bed when she was here yesterday."

"Peggy?" She blurted out the name. Immediately she admonished herself. The women in his life were none of her business.

"My sister comes to clean once a week for me," he replied. He'd tossed the fresh linens onto the bed and was now heading for the door. "I'm sure you can make your own bed. There's extra blankets on the shelf in the closet if you need them." Pausing as he stepped out into the hall, he turned back to her. "Your bathroom is the next door to the left. There's a linen closet inside with towels, washcloths, soap, et cetera. My room's at the other end of the hall, so you'll have your privacy. I'll set up your computer on the desk in the living room for now. If you can't work there, I'll move a table into the next bedroom down." He nodded to his right. "You can use that for an office."

Before she had a chance to respond, he was already on his way to the stairs.

"Whatever you say," she muttered to his departing back. For one brief moment, she'd actually thought he was going to show some friendliness, until he'd turned icy again. His determined dislike of her was wearing on her nerves. Forget about him, she ordered herself, and turned her attention to unpacking and making her bed.

She had just finished when heavy footsteps in the hall let her know Taggart was coming back.

"I've set steaks out to thaw for dinner," he informed her. "I'll be in my workshop if you need me. If you want to go for a walk, let me know and I'll come along."

Again she felt like the world's worst nuisance. "I didn't come up here to be a burden. I came up here because you gave me no choice."

He frowned impatiently, then his expression became shuttered. "Take the dogs along whenever you leave the house. Just say 'come' and they'll follow. They'll warn you of any predators, human or otherwise." He looked as if he was going to leave, then added, "I'd appreciate it if you didn't go far. If you get lost, just say 'home' and they'll lead you back."

Gillian frowned at him in confusion. She'd expected an argument from him, not a capitulation. "You are a constant surprise."

He shrugged. "I figure the quickest way to send you running is to make you feel suffocated or to force my presence on you. Then, like I've already told you, I'd have to go looking for you. I'm trying to save us both from unnecessary trouble. Besides, you couldn't ask for better protection than Goliath and Orion."

Again, before she could respond, he left. A minute later she heard the front door open and close.

Stepping out of her room, she expected to feel ill at ease in Taggart's home. After all, she was only there because he felt he had no alternative. Instead, she experienced an unexpected warmth and sense of security. It was something akin to slipping her feet into a pair of favorite slippers. The decor, though seemingly stark, appealed to

her. She'd always loved beautiful woods. Then there were
the paintings—real ones, not prints. Mountain landscapes, some of lakes surrounded by wilderness, some of
mountain meadows at sunset and others at sunrise, hung
on the walls. There was also a portrait of Taggart. The
eyes, she noted, held a surprisingly boyish, mischievous
glint. Clearly, the artist knew a side of him Gillian had
not been privy to.

Making a closer inspection, she saw the signature on
the landscapes, as well as the portrait, was that of an
Andrea Langley.

"Obviously a close friend of Taggart's," she muttered, again finding herself drawn to the portrait. A sensation that was very akin to jealousy caused her to frown.
He could have all the female friends he wanted, she assured herself. And she was not jealous because he'd
shown a pleasant side of himself to someone else. Her
reaction had merely been due to irritation at his attitude
toward her. She wasn't used to being made to feel like a
nuisance.

Pushing him from her mind, she went downstairs to
find her computer hooked up and ready for use. A fresh
pad of notepaper and a mug filled with pencils and pens
were beside it. Seating herself in front of the machine, she
switched it on and sought escape in her work. But she
could not concentrate on her story. Instead, her gaze
shifted from the computer screen to the huge window in
front of her and the panoramic view of the mountains
beyond.

When she tried to pull her attention back to her hero
and heroine, she found herself instead turning in her
chair and studying the surroundings of the room in which
she sat. It was as if she was trying to find clues to the inner man Taggart kept so well hidden from her. Glancing

at the clock, she realized she'd wasted an entire hour and groaned at her preoccupation with her reluctant host. "The man is making me crazy!" she seethed.

Suddenly the dogs started barking and she stiffened. Had her lunatic found her already? Panic curled through her. She took a couple of deep breaths and rose.

Above the barking she heard a vehicle approaching. Hurrying into the hall, she looked out one of the long windows on either side of the door. A Jeep pulled up and a handsome, tall, gray-haired woman in jeans, a blue plaid shirt and western boots climbed out. The dogs ran to greet her like an old friend, and Gillian relaxed. She stepped out onto the front porch as Taggart came striding out of his workshop.

"And to what do I owe this visit?" he asked the caller dryly, his tone implying he already knew the answer.

"I could lie and say I'd just been passing by and thought I'd stop by and check on your dogs to make certain your brother remembered to come feed them while you're gone," the woman replied, grinning broadly. "But then, I've never been good at lying. Truth is, I heard you had a houseguest and thought I'd come by and introduce myself."

Striding up onto the porch, she extended her hand to Gillian. "I'm Andrea Devereux, Taggart's mother. Wanda called to tell me you were coming up here and why. Thought I'd welcome you to our mountain. If you get bored here, go back down the drive and take the cut-off to the left—that'll take you to our place."

"Thanks," Gillian replied, accepting the woman's handshake. Unlike her son, Andrea Devereux made her feel welcome.

Andrea nodded, then headed back to her Jeep. "I wasn't sure if you two stopped in town for supplies, so I brought along a few staples from my freezer and some fresh vegetables from my garden."

Gillian followed. When the woman lifted a box of groceries off the passenger seat, she took it.

"I'll carry that inside," Taggart said, taking it from Gillian.

Where his hands had brushed hers, Gillian experienced an unexpected heat. Ignoring the sensation, she turned her full attention to Andrea. "Would you like some coffee?" she offered, glad of any company to take her mind off her enigmatic host.

"Love some," Andrea replied.

Gillian saw Taggart cast his mother a frown as if to say he wasn't seconding the invitation.

Andrea raised an eyebrow. "You've certainly become unsociable," she said. Disregarding his less than welcoming attitude, she followed him into the house.

"Sorry," he muttered contritely. "I've had a lot on my mind lately."

"Obviously," she replied, studying him closely.

Gillian had entered the kitchen behind Andrea and now she found herself the object of the older woman's scrutiny. The curiosity she'd seen when Andrea had first arrived had intensified.

"You'll be an interesting subject to paint," the woman said thoughtfully. "The coloring, the shape of your features . . . very nice. Warm."

Gillian suddenly realized who this woman was. "You're the one who painted the landscapes and the portrait of Taggart."

Andrea smiled. "Guilty as charged."

Gillian smiled back. "They're lovely. You've got a real talent. I can almost feel as if I'm in them, experiencing the place you've painted."

Andrea laughed. "I knew I liked you the minute I saw you. I'll look forward to painting you."

"You would really do a portrait of me?" Gillian had never felt so flattered.

"I always—"

"Mother," Taggart interrupted sharply, then in milder tones asked, "Did you bring some milk?"

"As a matter of fact I did," Andrea replied, pulling the carton out of the box he'd set on the table and handing it to him to be put in the refrigerator. Then, turning her attention back to Gillian, she finished, "I always paint people I find interesting."

Gillian had the strongest impression Taggart had been afraid his mother was going to say something else. She was certain she'd seen him cast a warning look at Andrea when he'd interrupted to ask about the milk. Then the truth dawned on her. More than likely, he was simply trying to discourage his mother from doing the portrait. He obviously didn't want any reminders of her once he'd freed himself of the responsibility he felt toward her.

Andrea glanced at her watch. "Actually, I have a couple of errands I need to run. I didn't realize how late it was." Already heading to the door, she glanced back at Gillian. "I'll see you again." Her voice held a promise. Then noticing that both Taggart and Gillian were beginning to follow, she held up her hand. "I can show myself out."

"I'll walk with you." Taggart's voice held no compromise. "Gillian, will you finish unloading the supplies?" he added, making it clear he wanted to speak to his mother alone.

"Sure," she replied, then had only a moment to bid Andrea goodbye as Taggart ushered the older woman hurriedly out of the room.

Unloading the box, she realized she was hungry. Wanda had insisted on fixing them an early lunch before they left to come up here, but at the time Gillian's stomach had refused food. She was washing an apple when Taggart returned.

"I'll be in my workshop," he informed her, then was gone again.

Taking a bite of the apple, she noticed her crystal was playing an unexpectedly cheerful note. "I've definitely got to work on your taste in men," she admonished it.

Chapter Seven

Gillian dropped her head in her hands and groaned. After Taggart's mother left, she'd returned to the living room and ordered herself to concentrate on her writing. She'd thought she was being successful until just now. Her brown-eyed hero suddenly had blue eyes and her description of those eyes matched Taggart's. Breathing an irritated sigh, she hit the backspace key on her computer and deleted the last sentence.

She was typing in a new description when the dogs began barking again. Grateful for any distraction as long as it wasn't her "fan," she went to the front door and peered out. Her crystal pealed a sour note as Harold's rental car came into view.

"You're right." Gillian touched it soothingly. "I could have lived happily without a visit from them, as well."

Evelyn waved as Gillian stepped out onto the porch. The dogs had positioned themselves in front of the car. When Harold started to step out, they ran, barking toward him, and he quickly closed the door and remained inside.

"Goliath. Orion. Friends. Sit," Taggart yelled, coming out of his workshop.

The dogs backed off but continued to watch the newcomers with interest.

Climbing out of the car, Evelyn stood, her gaze traveling over Taggart's house. "Nice little cabin in the woods," she said with a wide grin of approval.

"It's too secluded, if you ask me," Harold complained. As if he didn't quite trust their obedience, he kept a close eye on the dogs as he, too, exited the car. "It'd take the police half an hour to get here at top speed."

"But my dogs let me know if there's a stranger anywhere within smelling distance," Taggart countered.

He'd reached Goliath and Orion and was standing between them.

"Well, I know I'd feel safe with the three of you guarding me," Evelyn purred, moving toward the trio, her smile seductive. Coming to a halt just inches from Taggart, she grinned mischievously. "I may just have to find a maniac to pursue me." Then laughing lightly, she turned her attention to the dogs.

"Next to your master, you two are the handsomest bodyguards I've seen in a long time," she cooed, petting each in turn with lavish affection.

Both dogs' tails wagged and they nuzzled her playfully.

It would seem that male egos, be they human or dog, are susceptible to flattery by a pretty woman, Gillian mused acidly. *I'm really losing it!* she wailed silently. She was actually jealous that the dogs liked Evelyn. She wasn't jealous, she corrected, she'd just thought they would have better taste.

Giving the dogs each a final rub, Evelyn straightened and returned her full attention to Taggart. "I'd heard from Marigold that you were an excellent carpenter, but this place is magnificent. Did you built it all yourself?"

"Mostly," he replied.

She hooked her arm through his. "You'll have to give me the grand tour."

"Sure, why not?" Taggart replied.

Gillian had expected him to make an excuse and escape to his workshop. But apparently Evelyn had found the chink in his armor—his carpentry. Gillian recalled he'd even shown a momentary friendliness toward her when she'd admired his craftsmanship. In her case, however, his agreeableness had been fleeting. It would seem, she observed, that in Evelyn's case the effect was to be more long lasting. Her crystal struck a painfully sour note. If he succumbs to the woman's flattery, then he deserves what he gets, she told herself cynically.

"I'm especially interested in the master bedroom," Evelyn said as she and Taggart started toward the house. "I've always felt that it's the most important room in any home."

"Really, Evelyn," Harold admonished.

She glanced at him, her expression one of exaggerated innocence. "I'm simply repeating what friends of mine in real estate tell me is a major selling point of any house."

"I think we'll stick to seeing the living room today," Harold ordered.

Evelyn tossed him a disgruntled glance.

"Would you like some coffee?" Trained politeness had forced Gillian to make this offer. She hoped they'd refuse. In spite of her determination to remain indifferent to Taggart's personal life, she was finding Evelyn's constant clinging to him grating on her nerves.

"That sounds lovely," Evelyn replied.

Mentally kicking herself, Gillian forced a smile.

"Stay," Taggart ordered the dogs as he held the door open for Evelyn to enter. They returned to their guard positions while Gillian and Harold followed the others inside.

Taggart stopped at the entrance to the living room. "You can make yourselves comfortable in here. I'll set the coffee to brewing."

"I can at least see the kitchen," Evelyn insisted, refusing to release her hold on him. She glanced at Harold. "Surely you can't object to that."

He regarded her with a patronizing scowl, then shook his head and turned his attention to Gillian. "Your grandaunt told us of the scare you had this morning. I'd feel a great deal safer if you'd come back to California with us."

Taggart's gaze leveled on the man. "She's staying here."

Gillian saw Harold bristle. He wasn't used to having anyone exercise authority over him. If she'd thought that Taggart really wanted her there, she'd have been pleased. As it was, she simply preferred to avoid any confrontation. "You have to see the view from the deck." Taking Harold's arm, she guided him into the living room and toward the sliding glass doors on the far side.

"And we have coffee to brew," Evelyn reminded Taggart, giving his arm a gentle pull.

He nodded and led her to the kitchen.

"The man is a bully," Harold snarled as soon as he and Gillian were alone. "I hope you aren't letting him do your thinking for you."

Gillian paused in opening the sliding glass doors that led to the wide deck beyond and turned to face him. "I would never allow any man to do my thinking for me."

He smiled. "I'm glad to hear that."

She had to admit he sounded genuine. But then, she knew from experience Harold was a master manipulator. She recalled how he'd managed to make Ida do his bidding while causing her to think she was making her own decisions. It had taken Ida a long time to realize how controlled she was. But then her friend had been in love and hadn't minded succumbing to Harold's wishes until he'd pulled the reins in too tight.

Determined to change the subject, Gillian stepped out onto the deck. "Isn't this a great view?"

"The view is not important. Your safety is."

"I'm safe here," she assured him.

"I know you think you are, but I can't help worrying." He took her hands in his. "I'm driving back to Boston tonight. I have a morning meeting there, and then I'll be taking an afternoon flight to California. It's a business matter that just came up and has to be dealt with in person." He frowned toward the house. "I'm taking Evelyn with me. I had considered asking you to consider having her stay with you for added protection, but the way she's coming on to Devereux is embarrassing. Someone could be strangling you, and she'd never notice, she'd be too busy trying to seduce him."

"I heard that." Evelyn came around the corner of the house. "And that's not true. I'd do everything I could to make certain Gillian was okay." She glanced over her shoulder as Taggart too followed the porch around to join the others on the deck. "I simply enjoy flirting with handsome men. It's something I can't seem to control." Again, she hooked her arm through Taggart's as if staking a claim.

In spite of her order for it to remain silent regarding the Hyatts, Gillian's crystal insisted on issuing a single unpleasant peal.

Harold scowled at his sister. "You're coming back to California with me."

She smiled patronizingly. "Of course I am." Turning her gaze to Taggart, she breathed a regretful sigh. "I don't want to distract you from your duty. But as soon as Gillian is safe, I'll be back for the full tour."

Taggart merely smiled noncommittally. But behind his smile, Gillian noticed he was studying the woman speculatively. Well, if he'd decided that Evelyn was his type, then he was welcome to her, she told herself. She simply didn't want to be a witness. "I'll go see if the coffee has finished brewing." Before anyone could respond, she was on her way around the house to the kitchen.

To her relief, Harold insisted he and Evelyn remain only long enough for a single cup. But before leaving he attempted once again to convince Gillian to come back to California with him. Again she refused.

Following their departure, she was washing the coffee mugs when Taggart entered the kitchen. "Does Evelyn come on that strong all the time?" he asked.

The fact that he'd asked about Evelyn irritated her. "If you're trying to bolster your male ego, then consider it bolstered," she returned curtly. "The answer to your inquiry is no. I've seen her come on strongly but usually not this strongly." She told herself to be quiet. Instead her voice took on a cynical edge and she added, "Of course, her behavior could be due to the fact that you haven't succumbed to her charms. That could cause her to see you as a challenge she can't refuse. I don't think she's ever experienced rejection before."

He frowned out the kitchen window. "Women who play games make me uneasy." Still frowning, he headed to the door. "I'll be in my workshop."

A curl of guilt wove through Gillian. She had sounded shrewish. "I didn't mean to bruise your male ego," she said stiffly. "I'm sure Evelyn finds you very attractive."

He paused and turned back to face her. "My ego is undamaged," he assured her, then continued on out.

"But mine isn't," she muttered. Her mouth formed a pout. She was getting sick and tired of being treated like some homely mongrel who had ended up on his doorstep and he'd felt duty bound to take inside.

Up in her room, she made a critical appraisal of herself in the mirror. She looked frumpy. After the night she'd dressed in her suit, she'd reverted back to her wallflower look, partially from habit and partially because she'd had no desire to encourage Harold's attentions. But it hadn't dissuaded either lunatics or Harold.

Freeing her hair from the ponytail she'd gotten so used to keeping it in, she brushed it out and tied it back in a more gentle style with a ribbon. The jeans and sneakers stayed. She didn't want Taggart getting the idea she was pursuing him. She wasn't! She was doing this to make herself feel better.

The baggy shirt that was two sizes too big did get tossed. In its place she chose a light, summer sweater with short sleeves, a scoop neck and a fit that showed off her curves. It was pale green in color with tiny flowers embroidered on it and had always been one of her favorites. Making a second inspection of herself, she smiled.

She looked more like the woman she'd been before Ida's murder.

"Except maybe a little more strained around the eyes," she conceded, pulling out her makeup bag. A few light touches later, she gave herself a nod of approval and went downstairs to prepare dinner.

She'd put the potatoes in to bake and was beginning the salad when Taggart entered the kitchen.

"Sorry. I should have come in sooner to start dinner," he apologized. He halted in midstride. She'd fixed herself up. That sweater she was wearing was a real eye-catcher. Silently he groaned. He was only human. He didn't need this added enticement.

"I figured I'd do the cooking tonight. I'm not here for you to wait on me," she tossed back, continuing to concentrate on her preparations.

Getting out of the kitchen and away from her became his number one priority. "I'll set up the grill for the steaks."

She caught an underlying irritation in his voice. Glancing over her shoulder, she saw his jaw set in a hard, grim line. She'd known women who were possessive of their kitchens but she'd never expected Taggart to be. Setting aside the head of lettuce she'd just washed, she followed him out to the deck. "I didn't mean to overstep my bounds. I didn't know you were touchy about anyone else using your kitchen."

He tossed her a quizzical look. "My kitchen is your kitchen. I'm happy whenever anyone else does the cooking."

She scowled at him. "You didn't look happy just now." Another reason for his behavior crossed her mind. "I can assure you that I'm a good cook."

"I'm sure you are." *Didn't she know how tempting she looked?* he fumed. He was trying to keep his mind on business but she wasn't making it easy. "It's been a long day for both of us. I apologize if I was a little brusque when I came in. I've got a couple of orders I put off taking care of so that I could be at your grandaunt's house. I want to get them done. But right now I need to get this fire started."

His tone held dismissal, letting her know he wasn't interested in continuing a conversation with her. *And a pleasant good evening to you too,* she thought dryly, taking her cue and going back into the kitchen.

About the time she was putting the salad in the refrigerator to crisp, he returned to the kitchen. "The fire should be ready in half an hour. If the potatoes will be done by then, I'll be back to put the steaks on."

Gillian glanced at the clock. "They should be."

He nodded and left.

The realization that since she'd arrived here, he'd spent as little time as possible under the same roof with her occurred to her. "Like he said, he's got work to do," she reminded herself. Besides, what did she care how he spent his time? As long as he wasn't bothering her, she should be grateful.

But when the steaks were cooked, and she'd seated herself at the table to eat only to have him announce he was taking his dinner to his workshop, the sting of insult was too sharp to ignore. Watching his departing back, anger bubbled within her. She ate a bite of the steak. It landed like a rock in her stomach. "Enough is enough!" she growled, shoving her chair back and rising.

The two dogs jumped up as she descended from the porch. Flanking her, they accompanied her to within a few feet of the workshop, then lay down.

She didn't pause to knock on the door. Thrusting it open, she entered.

Taggart was seated at a high workbench. Jerking around, concern showed on his face. "What's wrong?"

"You're what's wrong!" she snapped. "As soon as my car's repaired, I'm leaving, and you're not coming along or following!"

The concern turned to impatience. "You're being unreasonable."

She glared at him. "You lied to me about not minding watching over me. A blind person a continent away could tell you dislike me. You can't even stand to be under the same roof with me." Pride caused her shoulders to straighten. "Well, that's your prerogative. Like you've already pointed out, some chemistries just don't mix. But I will not stay where I'm considered a nuisance." With a final glower at him, she stormed out and back to the house. The dogs, hanging back as if they sensed something was wrong, followed slowly, again resuming their guard position on the porch when she went inside.

Hoping someone who could fix her car immediately would be at the garage, she headed for the phone. Behind her she heard footsteps, then a hand closed around her arm. She looked up into Taggart's angry features.

His jaw tensed with purpose. "You're staying here."

"No, I'm not." She attempted to pull free but his hold remained firm. She glared at him. "I'll call daily to see if you've had any visions. That should satisfy your unwanted sense of duty toward me. Now let go!"

"Do you really want to know why I didn't eat with you tonight? Why I've been in my workshop all day? I'll tell you. It's because I find you distracting."

Gillian stopped her attempts to pull free. Again she'd seen the flash of heat in his eyes and there had been an underlying husky edge in his voice. "Distracting?"

"To guard you properly, I need to concentrate on your safety, not wonder how it would feel to kiss you."

Gillian smiled crookedly. "You were wondering that?"

"And a whole lot more," he admitted gruffly. Abruptly he released her. "Now eat your dinner," he ordered, already striding down the hall.

She heard the front door slam and knew he was angry with himself for having lost his temper and said more than he'd wanted to say. The smile on her face deepened. Her ego definitely felt a lot better.

As she again seated herself at the kitchen table, the small nudgings that had felt like jealously came back to taunt her. "So maybe I do find him appealing," she admitted between bites. Actually, there was no "maybe" about it. She pictured him in her mind and excitement spread through her.

"And so now what do I do?" she murmured speculatively. It could be that what she felt was simply lust. But then, didn't the majority of romantic relationships begin with a physical attraction? What would her heroine do under these circumstances? That was easy to answer. She would get to know him better.

As she stepped outside and her canine sentries came to flank her, she hesitated. She'd never been very good at flirting. But then she wasn't seeking him out to flirt. She merely wanted to make conversation . . . see if they had anything in common. Drawing a steadying breath, she continued on to his workshop. Again the dogs took their position a few feet from the door. She knocked, then entered without waiting for a response.

He was sanding what looked to be a leg for a table. Glancing over his shoulder, he frowned. "You didn't need to come back for the dishes. I'd have brought them up to the house later."

His voice held dismissal, but she stood her ground. "I was getting lonely up there. I thought maybe we could talk."

He stopped sanding and turned to her. "Talk about what?"

The impatience on his face caused her to falter, then she remembered the fire she'd seen in his eyes. Nothing ventured, nothing gained, she reasoned. "You do good work. I just wanted to see how it was done."

"I'm behind on my orders. I don't have time to give you a tour. Would you please go back to the house?" he requested stiffly.

Gillian scowled. "You really make it difficult for a person to get to know you."

He regarded her dryly. "I thought you'd determined that I was too arrogant and stubborn to be of any interest to you."

"I thought I'd give you a chance to prove me wrong."

Fire glimmered in his eyes. "As much as I'd like to take you up on that offer, this isn't the time."

Gillian flushed. "I didn't come down here to seduce you, if that's what you think."

"I'm not exactly sure what to think."

"I just thought we could be friends."

His gaze hardened. "Right now, it'd be best if we kept our relationship as impersonal as possible. Now, would you please go back up to the house?"

Clearly any distraction she caused him was a great deal weaker than he'd led her to believe. She felt like a fool...a rejected fool. "You can be truly insufferable, Taggart Devereux," she snarled.

She was halfway to the house when she remembered the dinner tray. She considered not going back, but she had something more to say to Mr. Devereux. Turning back, she saw him standing in the doorway watching her.

"I forgot the tray," she said curtly.

"I'll bring it up myself," he replied, his tone letting her know he didn't want her to return.

"I'm not like Evelyn. I don't go around trying to seduce every man I see. And I doubt we can be friends. Most likely we have nothing in common."

"Go inside," he ordered.

Tossing him a haughty glance, she obeyed.

Out of the corner of her eye she saw Goliath and Orion look at each other. They were clearly sensing the tension between the humans and wondering about taking sides. Then, as if to say they considered quarreling silly, they returned to their guard duties.

"I can't believe I owe my life to that cad," she seethed as she washed her dishes. "Cad" wasn't really a fair description, she admitted. He hadn't tried to take advantage of her.

She drew a tired breath. Wandering out onto the front porch, she sat down in one of the rocking chairs. Goliath rose, approached her and laid his head on her lap.

She petted him affectionately. "I owe your master my life," she said. "But I have to tell you, he's got to be one of the most aggravating men I've ever met."

Goliath merely wagged his tail and leaned into her hand to allow her to scratch his ear more efficiently.

Gillian frowned at the workshop, her inner vision filled with the image of the man inside. She hated being beholden to someone who treated her as if she was a thorn in his side.

Pushing him from her mind, she turned her gaze skyward. The heavens seemed larger and closer here in the mountains. A full moon cast an eerie glow over the landscape. "This was definitely a full moon kind of day," she murmured.

Catching movement out of the corner of her eye, she glanced earthward again and saw Taggart silhouetted in the doorway of his workshop. She could not see his face but she knew he was looking her way. She could sense his gaze as strongly as if it was a physical touch.

Abruptly, he stepped back and closed the door between them.

"I might as well be here alone," she told Goliath. "I certainly won't have any excuse for not getting a lot of work done." She gave the dog a final scratch behind the ear. "Thanks for the company." Then, easing herself out of the chair, she went inside and went to bed.

Chapter Eight

Gillian awoke the next morning feeling rested and re-
freshed. How she could have slept so soundly or so com-
fortably under Taggart's roof, she didn't understand. "It
was Goliath and Orion," she told herself as she climbed
out of bed and dressed. Knowing they were on guard had
eased her mind.

Taggart's strong form suddenly filled her mind. Well,
all right, knowing he was around probably helped, too,
she confessed grudgingly.

In the kitchen she found no sign that Taggart had risen
yet. Outside, the sun was cresting over the mountain. The
sky was clear, promising a beautiful day. She started the
coffee brewing, then went into the living room and turned
on her computer.

She'd intended to get right to work, but the thought of
pancakes taunted her. Back in the kitchen, she found the
ingredients and had just finished mixing a batch when
Taggart entered.

"I'm making pancakes," she informed him. Not wanting him to get the wrong idea yet again, she added stiffly, "I was hungry and mixing just enough for one seemed selfish. As long as the two of us are stuck here together, I figure we should try to make the best of it."

He merely nodded. "I'll set the table."

She noted his indifferent manner. While she had to confess to still being at least mildly embarrassed about their exchanges the night before, he'd obviously put them out of his mind. She would have preferred to ignore him as much as possible, but there was one thing she'd omitted saying since yesterday and she knew she had to say it. "Thank you for saving my life."

"I haven't saved it yet."

The fear she was trying to keep buried bubbled to the surface. "You could have just said 'you're welcome.' I'd really rather not think about that lunatic lurking out there plotting my demise."

Approaching her in one long stride, his hands closed around her upper arms. Anger etched itself into his features and he lifted her toward him, forcing her to stand on tiptoes. "I don't want you to ever forget he's out there. You have to be on your guard constantly."

The worry she saw behind his anger caused a rush of panic. Her jaw tensed. "I can't let fear rule my life," she growled as much to herself as to him.

He drew a harsh breath. As if just then realizing he was touching her, he loosened his hold until he was sure she was balanced, then released her and took a step back. "I don't want you to allow fear to rule," he said in a milder tone. "That can cause you to do irrational things. It's caution I want you to practice."

"I fully intend to do that."

He reached out and traced the line of her jaw with his finger. "I'm going to do everything in my power to keep you safe. But the images you inspire are—" he paused, then finished grimly "—difficult to sort through."

Her gaze narrowed on him. "There's something you're not telling me."

"Nothing that would be of any help," he replied and returned to setting the table.

Returning to her cooking, Gillian watched him out of the corner of her eye. He was infuriating. Still, she realized that when he was present she felt completely safe. "I know that as long as you're nearby, I won't be hurt." A flush tinted her cheeks when she realized she'd spoken aloud.

"Then I'll make certain I'm always nearby."

The protectiveness in his eyes caused a warmth to spread through her. He's doing this to keep his conscience free, not because he really wants to, she reminded herself curtly, and the warmth faded. Ordering herself to keep any future thoughts private, she returned to her cooking.

They ate breakfast in silence. Afterward, she insisted on doing the dishes while he took care of his dogs then returned to his workshop.

"Meanwhile, I shall enjoy the peace and quiet and get some work done," she told herself, sitting down at her computer. And for a while she was able to work. But as she finished a scene in which her heroine was so frustrated with the hero, the woman wanted to scream, she realized that her hero was taking on more and more of Taggart's characteristics. "The man's influence is insidious," she seethed.

Pushing back her chair, she rose, stretched and looked longingly out the window. The woods beckoned her. A walk would be a perfect way to clear her mind, she decided. Stepping out onto the front porch, she frowned at the workshop. Taggart had said she could go for a walk if she took the dogs along. But he'd also asked her to let him know when she left the house.

She started toward the workshop, then stopped. He might insist on accompanying her and his company was the one thing she didn't want. He was the reason she needed the walk in the first place. Between the dogs and her crystal, she should have plenty of warning of any danger, she assured herself.

"Come on, guys," she commanded her sentries.

Immediately they were on their feet, their tails wagging excitedly as if they'd been freed from captivity.

"I noticed a trail to the back," she said, petting Goliath and then Orion as they flanked her on either side. Their tails wagged even harder. Descending the steps, she headed around the house with her canine companions.

"And just where in the hell do you think you're going?"

At the sound of the angry male voice, Gillian turned to see Taggart approaching in long, purposeful strides. Her crystal played a dour note, confirming the anger she saw on his face. "So much for making a clean escape," she muttered under her breath. In louder tones, she said, "I was just going for a walk. You told me I could as long I had Goliath and Orion to protect me."

"I also asked you not to leave the house without informing me. I thought I had your word on that." Coming to a halt just inches from her, he glowered down at her.

"All right. You're right." She glowered back. "But I figured if I told you, you'd insist on coming along, and I didn't want to disturb your work. I wasn't planning to go far.''

An expression of indulgence replaced his anger. ''I could use some fresh air. Lead the way.''

Gillian was tempted to return to the house, but she knew she'd simply spend the next hour pacing the floor. Rewarding him with an indulgent look of her own, she continued toward the path she'd spotted earlier.

Suddenly his hand closed around her arm and she was jerked to an abrupt halt. Neither the crystal nor the dogs were issuing any warning. ''What . . .'' she started to demand impatiently, but the haunted look in his eyes caused the rest of her protest to die in her throat.

''I don't want you on this path.'' It was an order. ''If you want to go for a walk, we can go down the road.''

A chill of fear traveled through her. ''Did you see something?''

''You lying at the base of a tree several yards further on.''

Her fear intensified. ''Maybe I'll just go back inside.''

He nodded his approval and released her. ''I'll come with you.''

The urge to run was strong, but she forced herself to walk at a normal pace to the house. Reaching the porch, she noted that the dogs still showed no sign they sensed danger. Her crystal was humming a low note, but that, she knew, was due to Taggart. ''Whatever is going to happen is not going to happen today,'' she said aloud, more to calm herself than to inform Taggart of her supposition.

''No, not today,'' he confirmed. ''But soon.''

Entering the house, she recalled a scene she'd witnessed several days earlier. ''Does Chief Brant know of your ability? I was just remembering the first time we called him to my grandaunt's house. When he was leaving and you and he were on the porch, he asked if there was anything you knew that he should know. At the time, I thought he thought I'd left something important out when I'd told him about getting the letter.''

Taggart shrugged. ''I've never told him about my precognitive experiences. I have showed up a couple of times when I knew he needed a helping hand, but I doubt he suspects anything. At least, he's never said anything about my unexpected appearances being too much of a coincidence. Thatcher's got both feet planted pretty solidly on the ground. I figure if I told him, he'd start looking at me as if my elevator didn't go all the way to the top floor.''

''Probably,'' Gillian agreed.

''You're safe in here,'' he said abruptly. ''I'm going back to my workshop.'' He started to leave, then paused. ''Just as a precaution, I'll make certain all the doors are locked before I leave.''

Gillian wanted to ask him to stay, but pride refused to allow that. ''Thanks,'' she said stiffly.

For a long moment he studied her, then asked, ''Do you play gin rummy?''

''I've played a couple of times.''

''We'll play at the table on the deck. That way you can get your fresh air in safety.''

She knew he'd read her fear and was attempting to appease her. The words to tell him that she would be fine on her own made it all the way to the tip of her tongue but that was as far as they got. She wanted company and his was all that was available. ''If you're certain a break won't put your production schedule behind by too far, I'd enjoy the diversion.''

"A break isn't going to make any difference," he assured her. "I'll get the cards."

A few minutes later, watching him as he dealt out the first hand, Gillian noticed his jaw tensing. This time her pride refused to allow her to remain silent. "It's pretty clear you don't want to play cards with me. You're having to fight to keep a reasonably pleasant expression on your face. I suggest you go work. I can entertain myself."

"It's not that I mind playing cards with you." He frowned self-consciously. "The problem is, I'm having trouble sorting through the variety of images involving you that keep popping into my mind. Some are downright lecherous." The expression of a man angry with himself for having said more than he should again spread over his face. "After all, you're an attractive woman, and I'm only human. But these mental wanderings are interfering with the precogs I need to save your life."

In spite of his irritation with himself, she saw a heat in his eyes he was unable to smother. A responding heat began to spread through her. The last time this happened, you ended up being rejected, she reminded herself. Keep your distance. Instead, she heard herself saying, "Maybe you should tell me about the lecherous ones."

"I think not."

He looked uneasy, as if afraid he was in danger of losing control of the situation. A sense of womanly power filled her and she smiled. "I've had a few lecherous thoughts about you, myself. We could compare notes. Consider it research . . . the male idea of lecherous versus the female idea of lecherous. It could be very beneficial to my work." A part of her was stunned. She'd never flirted so overtly with a man before, but then she'd never meet anyone who affected her like Taggart. He could make her so angry she wanted to scream, and still she found herself being irresistibly drawn to him.

A scowl descended over his features. "That kind of research is going to have to wait. Right now, I have to concentrate on keeping you alive. Now pick up your cards."

Protest bubbled up within her and a mischievous gleam sparked in her eyes. "I never thought I'd hear myself saying this, but you actually look sort of cute with that frown on your face. Of course, it could be that I've seen it so often, I'm not intimidated any longer."

His jaw tensed. "Gillian, behave. This is serious. Now pick up your cards."

Embarrassment flowed through her. He'd spoken to her as if she was a disobedient child. She'd made a fool of herself again. Whatever thoughts he was having obviously didn't run very deep, and she felt certain he had no intention of ever acting on them. To add to her humiliation, she'd proved to be a terrible flirt. She hadn't even been able to get him to smile. Even Evelyn had made him smile. "I think I'll go work."

He made no attempt to stop her as she rose and went into the house.

Sitting down in front of her computer, she assured herself that this attraction she was feeling for Taggart was merely a passing fancy. He'd saved her life once already. She saw him as her protector. "When this is all over, I'll wonder what I ever found so attractive about him," she murmured.

At that moment a movement caught her attention. Looking up, she saw him walk by the window. Well, maybe she wouldn't have to wonder too hard, she conceded. "It's just physical," she grumbled, and ordered herself to concentrate on her story.

To her dismay, Taggart didn't go back to his workshop. Instead, he spent the remainder of the day in his study. He did eat his lunch while he worked, thus allowing her to avoid his company. Still, as hard as she tried to ignore his close proximity, she was acutely aware of his presence.

But it was dinner that proved to be the real strain. During the meal neither spoke except when necessary. Gillian, still embarrassed by her unskilled flirting, guessed Taggart was afraid of saying anything that might encourage her amateurish attempts to interest him once again. By the time the meal was over her nerves were brittle. "You cooked, I'll clean," she said.

He left without an argument. She had carried the dishes to the sink and was returning to the table to get the glasses, when he strode back in.

Coming to a halt only inches from her, his hands closed around her upper arms. "I gave my word to your grandaunt that I would behave like a gentleman. I vowed to myself that I would keep you alive. I promise you that when this is over we're going to have a very serious discussion about our lecherous thoughts."

Before she could think of anything to say, his mouth found hers. A fire flamed to life within her. Her heart pounded. Her blood raced. Then abruptly she was freed.

Feeling deserted and shaken, she stood mutely as he made a hasty exit. "That's definitely something to look forward to," she murmured, when she could finally think once again. The urge to run after him and insist on having that talk now was strong, but she'd seen the determination on his face and knew it would be futile.

A smile of anticipation tilted the corners of her mouth and she returned to cleaning the kitchen.

Chapter Nine

Gillian awoke slowly, a soft smile on her face. She'd been having the most stimulating dream about being in Taggart's arms. "I really don't see any reason to wait until this is over before he and I get to know each other a little better," she mused, a purposeful gleam in her eyes. An evening curled up beside him on the couch watching television or reading or, better still, quietly watching a fire blazing in the hearth would certainly beat spending an evening with her computer in the living room while he remained in his study.

Tossing the covers off and rising, she realized that for the first time since the letters had begun, she was actually looking forward to facing the day.

Taggart was seated at the picnic table on the deck, his back to her. As she approached, she envisioned herself placing her hands on his shoulders and gently leaning against him to peer down at whatever had him so absorbed. Just the thought caused a rush of excitement.

"Morning," he said stiffly, abruptly rising before she reached him.

"Morning." She smiled, hoping for an answering smile.

He frowned. "I don't like that look on your face. I've seen it on women's faces before, just before they go after unsuspecting male prey."

She regarded him dryly. "Surely you can't consider yourself 'unsuspecting'?"

"I thought I'd made it clear that I need you to keep your distance if I'm to protect you."

Gillian breathed a regretful sigh. "You do make difficult rules." A coaxing quality entered her voice. "Are you sure we can't bend them just a little?"

He held both hands up in front of him as if warding off an approaching menace. "Absolutely. Now would you please behave?"

"I haven't misbehaved yet."

"Let's just keep it that way."

The resolute set of his jaw told Gillian he wasn't going to let her get physically close to him. But that didn't mean she couldn't get to know him better, she reasoned, and his work was a good place to start. Her gaze shifted to the table. An assortment of woodworking tools lay in disarray on either side of a rectangular piece of smoothed wood, squared at one end and curved at the other. He'd been working a leaf design, similar to the one on her bed, into the curved section of the wood. "What are you making?" she asked, approaching the table for a closer look.

"It's the headboard of a cradle."

She glanced toward him to see him frowning worriedly at the piece on the table. "It looks very nice," she said encouragingly, wondering what he could find so wrong. Admittedly it was unfinished, but what he'd done so far looked perfect to her.

"I shouldn't be working on it. I've got other things more important at the moment I should be concentrating on."

Unable to stop herself, she touched the wood. "I'm sure whoever you're making this for considers it a priority item."

His expression darkened. "It could be a premature task."

Concern for the mother and child for whom the cradle was being constructed filled her. "Is there a problem with the pregnancy?"

A sudden burst of excited barking split the air, cutting off his response. In the next instant she saw Goliath and Orion come dashing around the house and into the woods. At the same time, her crystal issued a piercing warning note.

"It's probably just a rabbit. But I want you in the house until I check it out," Taggart ordered.

Gillian's hand closed around the crystal. Silently, she ordered it to be still so she could think. But fear for Taggart consumed her mind. "I'm certain it's not a rabbit. You can't go out there alone."

"If it is your 'fan', he's not after me. Now get inside."

Knowing arguing would be futile, she obeyed. But she kept the glass door open and remained just on the other side of the remaining screened barrier.

"Goliath! Orion!" Taggart called, quickly making his way off the deck and to the edge of the woods.

Gillian could hear the dogs in the distance. Suddenly their barking turned to distressed yapping. She knew without a doubt that they'd been injured. Guilt flowed through her. If they'd been hurt because of her, she'd never forgive herself.

The sound of brush crunching underfoot caught her attention. Taggart was now running into the woods and he was taking the same path she'd started to walk yesterday—the path he'd ordered her to stay away from. More certain than ever that the harm the dogs had encountered had been meant for her, she refused to allow Taggart to face whatever or whoever was out there alone. In the next instant she was dashing off the deck and down that same path.

Rounding a bend, Gillian saw Taggart and the two dogs ahead. Goliath and Orion were rubbing their faces in the leaves and underbrush as if trying to rid themselves of something unpleasant they'd stuck their noses in. Taggart was kneeling beside them, trying to calm them so that he could examine them.

"What's happened?" Gillian demanded.

Her crystal issued a loud peal of alarm.

Taggart jerked around, his expression one of shock. "Get down!" He lunged for her, catching her by the waist and falling to the ground with her. She heard a swish, then a thud followed by a twang. Looking upward, she saw an arrow embedded in the tree she'd been standing by. Taggart, she recalled, had mentioned seeing her lying at the base of a tree. Clearly she'd found the right one.

"You were supposed to stay at the house," he growled, continuing to use his body to shield her.

"I refuse to cower in the background while others are being harmed because of me," she returned in her defense.

Taggart scowled darkly. Never taking his eyes off her, he yelled, "Goliath. Orion. Home!"

The dogs each let out a low, long whine, then obeyed.

His face only inches from hers, he said with harsh command, "Now for you. You do exactly what I say."

Gillian could feel his anger like a physical force. She nodded.

"On the count of three, we're going to run for the house. Keep low. Don't look back. Don't stop until you're inside and lying behind the couch. One..."

Gillian's hand closed around his arm. "You're coming with me, right? You're not going crashing off into the woods as a diversion or seeking the nut who shot at me?"

"I'm coming with you. Going looking for this guy right now would be stupid. He has the advantage. He knows where we are. We have no idea where he is."

Gillian breathed a sigh of relief. "Let's go then."

"One. Two. Three."

Gillian was on her feet running. As Taggart had instructed, she kept bent low. She was aware of him running beside her, keeping pace with her, and realized he was maintaining a position that would shield her. More worried for him than for herself, she forced herself to move faster.

Reaching the door, her hands were shaking so badly and she was gasping so hard for breath, she couldn't get the door latch to give. He reached around her, flung it open and shoved her inside. Managing to round the couch, she fell on the floor behind it.

"Stay there," he ordered.

"Where are you going?" she demanded.

"I'm going to make a quick check of the perimeter."

As he disappeared into the kitchen, fear for him threatened to overwhelm her. Remembering the phone in the hall, she mentally counted to three, then made a dash for it. Huddled beside a large bench and keeping an eye on the front door, she punched in the emergency number for the police. Forcing herself to speak calmly, she told Chief Brant what had occurred.

"Gillian!" It was Taggart. He sounded panicked.

"I'm in the hall," she called back. He came through the doorway as she was hanging up. "I just called Thatcher. He'll be here as fast as possible. He's calling in a few extra men and having someone, I can't remember who, bring their hunting dogs."

Taggart went down on his knees in front of her, anger replacing his panic. "You are the most hard-headed woman I've ever met. Why can't you follow orders? I've tried reasoning with you. I've tried fear. I've even tried cajoling you. Nothing works."

She grinned impishly. "I don't remember any cajoli—" A very unpleasant truth dawned on her and her grin vanished. "Are you telling me that kiss, your claim of 'lecherous thoughts', all that was merely an attempt to keep me in line?"

"I'm trying to keep you alive," he growled.

She felt like a complete idiot. "You manipulative chauvinist. You thought one little kiss would make my brain turn to mush, and I'd follow your every command. Well, you can just take your male ego—"

"We can discuss what I can do with my ego later," he cut her short. "Right now I want to get my dogs to the vet and you away from here."

She heard Goliath and Orion whimpering on the front porch and again guilt assailed her. "I don't want you hurt because of me. You take the dogs. I'll find a place to hide until Thatcher gets here."

"You're coming with me. If you don't want to get anyone else hurt, this time you'll do exactly what I say."

The determined line of his jaw let her know he wasn't going to leave without her. The dogs whimpered again. "All right," she agreed through clenched teeth.

"I'm going to pull the truck up as close to the porch as possible. As soon as I have the dogs in the back, I'll get in behind the wheel. That's when I want you to make a dash for the passenger side. As soon as you're inside, get down out of view. Have you got that?"

She hated continuing to accept his aid but common sense prevailed over her pride. "I've got it."

Gillian followed him to the door.

"Don't make yourself an easy target. He'll expect you to be standing, so crouch as much as possible when you run," he instructed. "While you're waiting, keep the door open just a crack so you can see what's going on. That way you'll know when to make your run. Also keep an eye on the perimeter of the yard just in case he shows himself."

As angry as she was with him, Gillian grabbed at his arm when he started to step out onto the porch. "Maybe we should wait until Thatcher gets here."

"Just do what I say. This isn't my time to die."

She continued to clutch his sleeve. "You could be wrong."

"Maybe, but I trust my instincts and I intend to follow them." Taking her by the wrist, he forced her to release him. In the next instant, he was out the door and on his way to his truck.

Following his instructions, Gillian crouched low but kept her body at the ready. If he needed her help she was determined to give it. In front of her she saw his dogs. They were lying on the porch, making sounds of distress while rubbing at their noses and eyes with their legs and paws. The urge to comfort them was strong, but she knew her aid could place them in even more danger.

Moving swiftly, Taggart dropped the tailgate of the truck. Then sliding in behind the wheel, he quickly backed the vehicle up to the porch.

"Goliath. Orion. In," he ordered.

The dogs, now obsessed with their misery, didn't obey.

Cursing under his breath, he jumped from the cab. Reaching Orion first, he grabbed the smaller dog and quickly put him in the bed.

Gillian didn't wait for her cue. She knew he couldn't easily lift Goliath on his own. When he reached for the bigger dog, she was there lifting, as well. Together, they got Goliath into the bed in one smooth motion.

"Get in!" he yelled at her, slamming the tailgate shut with a noise that echoed through the woods.

By the time he was behind the wheel, she was in the cab, her head down on the seat. She heard gravel spraying and felt the truck fishtail. Then they were moving down the road, taking the curves at a speed that at one moment was pressing her against the door, and in the next, forcing her head against Taggart's leg.

Reaching the main road, he slowed. To her relief she heard a police siren in the distance. As it drew nearer, Taggart pulled off onto the shoulder and stopped.

"Keep your head down," he growled when she started to sit up and look out.

Reluctantly, she obeyed.

The siren reached them, then it was shut off and she knew Thatcher had stopped, as well.

"Stay down and out of sight," Taggart ordered, climbing out of the cab.

She started to protest.

"It'll be safer for all of us," he added curtly, and again she reluctantly obeyed.

She heard him describing to Thatcher where the attack had taken place.

"I've got men and dogs coming," Thatcher said when Taggart had finished. "We'll scour your mountain, but it's my guess the guy is gone by now. Probably regrouping and planning another form of attack. Can't believe he used a bow and arrow."

"He's proficient with the weapon. If I'd moved one millisecond slower, he'd have hit Gillian. And tell your dog handlers to keep an eye on their animals. The guy's got Mace, and he's using it to cause harm."

The sound of other cars stopping drowned out some of the rest of Taggart and Thatcher's conversation. Gillian heard other men's voices joining theirs, then Taggart was climbing back into the cab.

"I'm going to drop you off at the police station while I take the dogs to the vet," he said, pulling back onto the road. "You're to stay inside and out of sight."

"Maybe you'd like for me to crawl under one of the desks," she suggested dryly.

"That's a thought."

Rewarding him with a disgruntled grimace, she eased herself into a sitting position.

When he frowned at her, she frowned back. "I really think we're far enough away."

He didn't argue.

A sudden worry occurred to her. "Shouldn't we warn your parents there's a lunatic in the woods?"

"Thatcher will send someone to warn them. But they're in no danger. I'd know if they were."

There was a positiveness in his voice that assured Gillian this was true. Breathing a sigh of relief, she fell silent for the remainder of the ride.

A short while later, as they entered the police station, Wanetta Jones, the dispatcher, greeted them with a smile. "Don't worry," the young, dark-haired, dark-eyed woman said with assurance. "I can protect Gillian." She patted the gun on her hip, then nodded toward the case of rifles on the walls. "I'm proficient with both."

Taggart scanned the room. "You're the only one here?"

"The chief and deputy are out at your place." Wanetta's shoulders squared. "You don't have to worry about Gillian. I can look after her."

"As long as she behaves herself," Taggart qualified, making it clear he did not doubt the policewoman's abilities, that it was Gillian's behavior that worried him. His gaze narrowed on her. "You will do what Wanetta says."

The hairs on Gillian's neck bristled, but before she could tell him he had no right to talk to her like a child, he turned to the dispatcher. "Don't let her set foot outside of this place. I'll be back as soon as I've gotten my dogs taken care of."

Without giving either of them a chance to question his orders, he left.

"I can sure understand why Taggart's never married," Wanetta said, as the door swung closed behind him. "Who'd want to be bossed around like that? Not even a please or thank you. Just do as I say."

"He's had a difficult day, and he's concerned about his dogs." Gillian mentally gasped. She'd defended Taggart! Well, he had saved her life, she reminded herself grudgingly. She owed him for that.

"My dad can get real down when one of his dogs is sick," Wanetta admitted. The switchboard buzzed, demanding her attention. Hurrying to answer it, she said, "It'd be best if you waited in the chief's office. There aren't any windows in there."

Not wanting to give credence to Taggart's implication that she was difficult, Gillian immediately did as she was asked.

Alone in Thatcher's office, she sank into a chair and stared unseeingly at the wall in front of her. "I can't believe this is happening to me," she muttered. To her knowledge, romance writers did not usually attract violent fans. Even more, the chances of both her and Ida being singled out by a lunatic had to be astronomical.

The remembered swish of the arrow as it flew past her brought a chill of fear. Trying not to think about it, she closed her eyes and attempted to plot her next chapter. This escape didn't work. By the time Taggart returned, she was pacing the floor.

"I can't live like this... being in fear of stepping outside," she told him as they started back to his place. She glanced through the rearview mirror into the empty bed of the truck. Both of the dogs had received an extra heavy dose of spray in the eyes. The vet was certain they would recover fully but he'd insisted on keeping them at his place for a couple of days. "And I don't want any other living thing harmed because of me."

"Then I'd suggest you follow my instructions to the letter."

"I did and your dogs still got hurt."

Taggart's jaw tensed. "I'm not in the mood to argue with you."

"You'd better not be considering trying cajoling or you'll find yourself in more danger from me than from my fan," she warned.

"I was hoping you'd cooperate because it's the sensible thing to do."

Impatience laced his voice, giving the impression he was beginning to believe she was incapable of being sensible. Again the hairs on her neck bristled. But when she glanced toward him and saw the tired, worried lines in his face, her anger subsided. They were both unwilling victims—she of a deranged stalker, and he, of an innate talent. "I'm trying."

"I know this isn't easy for you," he said gruffly. "But we'll see it through together."

And then our paths will part, hopefully never to cross again, she finished silently for him. And that suited her just fine.

Thatcher was waiting for them when they returned to Taggart's house. The dogs, he informed them, hadn't been any help in finding the attacker's trail. Her archer had sprayed his arrow with Mace to cover any scent he might have left on it. Without an odor to follow, the animals had been confused about what they were to hunt for. They'd ended up chasing rabbits.

"The arrow was high tech, designed for killing," he told them. "Looks like you could use some help up here. I'm going to deputize a couple of men, put them on twelve hour shifts to help watch over Gillian."

"I don't want anyone else placed in danger because of me," she protested. "I wouldn't even be here with Taggart, but he gave me no choice."

"These men will know how to protect themselves," Thatcher assured her.

Gillian read the resolve on the chief's face. "I appreciate your concern," she said with resignation.

But while Taggart walked Thatcher to his car, she paced the living room floor. When he returned to the house, she met him in the hall. "The town can't afford to provide a private guard for me for any length of time. Besides, I can't stay here indefinitely. There has to be another way. I can seek out secluded, hard-to-find places. Or just keep moving. I'll call every day. You can tell me what to avoid or if I'm safe where I am for a while."

"The next attempt is going to happen within the next couple of days," he replied.

A chill came over her. "How can you be so certain?"

"I just know."

She saw the haunted look in his eyes. "You've had another vision."

"This time we're going to nail this guy," he vowed.

She felt nausea building. "I'm scared."

"You should be."

She frowned. "You could have said something a little more comforting than that."

"I want you to understand how dangerous a position you're in."

"I do."

"Good. Now maybe you'll follow instructions." His gaze shifted to the entrance to the living room. "I'm going to move your computer up to your room. I don't want you in the living room unless I'm with you."

Her legs suddenly felt weak. "Is that where it happens?"

Approaching her in one long stride, he captured her face in his hands. "That's where it's *not* going to happen."

The heat from his touch spread a warmth through her and she knew he would do everything in his power to protect her. And then he'd be glad to be rid of her, she reminded herself. Pride forced her to step back, breaking free from the contact. "There's a table in my bedroom that should do."

His expression cold with purpose, he nodded.

Gillian had just gotten her machine back into working order and was arranging her papers on the table when she heard a car in the distance. The chief had wasted no time, she thought. Out of politeness, she decided she should go downstairs and introduce herself to the deputy.

Midway down the staircase, she saw Taggart already at the door. He held his hand up to stop her approach and she froze. Surely her murderer wouldn't come knocking, she thought, but still she'd promised to obey him, and this time she would.

Her crystal issued a long, low note of discord, and she tensed. "Be careful," she warned Taggart.

He glanced up at her questioningly.

"My crystal doesn't like whoever is coming," she replied.

He nodded. His body tensed for action, he peered out the window.

Gillian heard the car park and the door open. As if he couldn't believe what he was seeing, Taggart shook his head, then, with an impatient scowl, he opened the door and stepped out onto the porch.

The crystal chimed in distaste.

"I just couldn't stay away." It was Evelyn's voice.

Silently agreeing with her crystal's reception, Gillian ordered it to be quiet as she continued down the stairs.

She reached the front door at the same time Evelyn mounted the porch.

"You're looking as good as ever," the woman cooed at Taggart, then her gaze shifted to Gillian and the smile that had been on her face vanished. "You, however, look absolutely awful."

"What are you doing here?" Gillian asked bluntly, peering past Evelyn, expecting to see Harold, as well.

"If you're looking for my brother, he's in California." Evelyn's chin firmed. "I'm here because I just couldn't walk away. I've always felt guilty that I wasn't able to be there to save Ida. Harold would be just devastated if something happened to you. So I'm here to offer my services."

"Gillian is being well looked after," Taggart assured her.

Evelyn placed her hand on his arm and felt the muscles. A seductive glimmer entered her eyes. "I'm sure she is." Then her expression became businesslike once again. "However, one of my former male friends was an expert in karate. He taught me a few moves. I can take care of myself and I can help take care of Gillian." Her mouth formed a coaxing pout. "Please, you've just got to let me stay. I'm determined to help watch over dear Gillian. If you won't allow me to remain in the house, I'll be forced to camp out in my car, and I'll probably get the most dreadful cramp in my neck."

Gillian had to fight to keep the impatience out of her voice. "That really isn't necessary."

"I know you've got Taggart and his dogs..." Evelyn paused and glanced around. "By the way, where are Goliath and Orion?"

"They're at the vets." It was Taggart who answered. "Someone sprayed them with Mace." His voice promised reprisal.

Evelyn again placed a hand on his arm, this time as a gesture of sympathy. "I'm so sorry to hear that."

That the woman couldn't seem to keep her hands off of Taggart grated on Gillian's nerves. "It's really not safe for you to be here."

Abruptly, as if a sudden realization had dawned on her, Evelyn's gaze swung back to Gillian. "Was there another attempt on your life?"

"Someone shot at her with a bow and arrow," Taggart replied, before Gillian had a chance to respond.

"You really should go home. I wouldn't want you accidentally harmed in my place," Gillian added quickly. "Besides, the chief is sending a couple of deputies to help Taggart."

"My safety is unimportant." Evelyn turned to Taggart. "You will let me stay, won't you?"

He shrugged. "Sure, why not?"

Gillian couldn't believe her ears. She'd been certain he'd send Evelyn packing. Instead, he'd capitulated without even a hint of argument.

"Wonderful." Evelyn beamed. "I'll just go get my bags."

"It's really not safe for you—" Gillian began to repeat her earlier objection.

"You should be getting back in the house," Taggart ordered, cutting her short.

The resolute set of his jaw let her know he intended to make the decisions about who would go and who would stay. *I guess women who play games make him uneasy, but not that uneasy,* she thought cynically. Then, of course, he wasn't above playing games himself, she recalled. Tossing him an angry glance, she went inside.

"So I look absolutely awful?" she grumbled under her breath, still smarting from Evelyn's blunt greeting. Passing the hall mirror, she glimpsed herself. She did look pretty bad. The stress of the day had deepened the lines of her face, her complexion was pale and her hair a mess. "All right, so I haven't taken the time to put myself in order. Well, I've had a lot on my mind," she defended, continuing up to her room.

Behind her, she heard Taggart helping Evelyn with her luggage. Gillian quickened her pace, escaping into her room before they reached the landing.

"You can use this room," she heard Taggart saying. "I'll get you some sheets and pillowcases." From the hall came the sound of the linen closet being opened.

"Why don't you help me make my bed?" Evelyn coaxed.

"You're a big girl. I'm sure you can handle that job on your own," he replied.

"But everything is so much more fun with two than one," she persisted.

From outside came the sound of another car approaching.

"That'll be the deputy. I need to go let him in," Taggart said, already heading down the hall.

Gillian heard Evelyn's exaggerated sigh of regret, then came a light, playful laugh, followed by the closing of a door.

"I cannot believe I've been eavesdropping," she admonished herself, forced to confess she'd been leaning against her bedroom door to hear better. Taggart had duped her. Why she was even the least bit interested in any of his amorous pursuits was beyond her comprehension. "They deserve each other," she muttered.

Feeling as if the walls were closing in on her, she went downstairs to introduce herself to the deputy.

"You've got a second woman here?" an unfamiliar and yet in some vague way familiar male voice was asking as she descended the stairs.

"It seemed like the right thing to do," Taggart replied.

Halfway down the stairs, Gillian stopped. The second man was dressed in jeans, a shirt and Western-cut boots, much like Taggart, but that was not where the similarity ended. He was older but the face was very close to the same.

Spotting her, he smiled. "You have to be Gillian. Mother described you perfectly."

"This is my brother, Simon," Taggart introduced the new arrival. "He's the deputy."

"Pleased to meet you," she replied automatically, still recovering from the shock of seeing a near duplicate of Taggart.

Simon's smile warmed even more. "The pleasure's all mine."

The urge to immediately like him was strong, but she'd learned her lesson the hard way with Taggart. She'd keep her distance from the Devereux men. A coolness descended over her features as she continued down the stairs. "I'm really sorry to be causing so much inconvenience to everyone," she said with stiff politeness.

Simon gave Taggart a questioning look. "Don't tell me you've already managed to alienate Miss Hudson?"

Taggart shrugged. "It wasn't difficult. She can be stubborn."

Simon again smiled at Gillian. "I hope you won't judge me by my brother's behavior. May I call you Gillian?"

His openly friendly manner was much too infectious to resist. This time she couldn't stop herself from smiling back. "Yes, of course."

"My cup runneth over." Evelyn's voice sounded from behind Gillian. "Another handsome man. I should have come for a visit a long time ago."

"This is Evelyn Hyatt, a friend of Gillian's from California. Evelyn, this is my brother, Simon." Taggart made the introductions.

"Now I'm in a real muddle." Evelyn's gaze roamed slowly over Simon. "I can't decide which of you to choose for the main course and which to have for dessert."

Simon raised an eyebrow in Taggart's direction, as if again questioning his brother's judgment, then said, "I'm going to have a look around outside. You children behave yourselves."

"Looks like you get to be both courses." Evelyn wrapped her arm around Taggart's.

"For the time being, we need to concentrate on Gillian's safety." Taggart gently but firmly freed himself. "I'm going to get dinner started."

Watching Evelyn in action was setting Gillian's already-strained nerves on edge. "I'll help," she said firmly, adding with even more command, "Evelyn, you can relax. Go enjoy the view from the deck."

"Sounds like Gillian wants a few words in private with you, Taggart." Mischief sparked in Evelyn's eyes and she turned to Gillian. "I'm sorry if I've been stepping on your toes. You did lead me to believe there was nothing between you and Taggart."

"There is nothing," Gillian assured her curtly.

"Still, you two seem to have something you need to talk about, and I do hate confrontations." A catlike grin spread over Evelyn's face. "I think I'll help Simon check the perimeter."

"I'd suggest you stay inside. I wouldn't want Gillian's pursuer to mistake you for her," Taggart warned.

Evelyn regarded him dryly. "A blind man couldn't mistake us." Apology spread over her face, and she quickly turned to Gillian. "Not that you aren't attractive in your own darling little way." Clearly believing she'd smoothed the waters, she returned her attention to Taggart and smiled sweetly. "But I appreciate your concern. I do think I'll stay inside and rest for a while. I've had a long drive today."

"A blind man..." Gillian muttered under her breath, preceding Taggart into the kitchen.

As soon as they were alone, she turned to him. "Evelyn is not my 'friend.' The only reason she's even willing to give me the time of day is because she'd do anything to please her brother. You're the one who invited her to stay." She meant to stop there, but heard herself adding, "I was under the impression you didn't like her any more than I do. Obviously, where women are concerned, you can't be trusted."

Unexpectedly, a crooked smile tilted one corner of his mouth. "You're cute when you're jealous."

Embarrassment brought a flush to her cheeks. "I am not jealous. If you want to have an affair with Evelyn that's fine with me." A bitter taste filled her mouth. She knew she was lying. She did care. The man had made a fool of her, she reminded herself curtly. Still, the thought of him and Evelyn together caused her stomach to knot. "This is your house and you can allow whomever you wish to stay. But I can't abide that woman, and I won't be cloistered here with her. I'd rather take my chances on my own." She headed for the door, determined this time to be on her way.

"You're not going anywhere outside of this house without me." Capturing her by the arm, he brought her to a halt. "Evelyn showed up, and she's one determined woman. I didn't see much choice but to let her stay." Exasperation showed on his face. "I would have thought this morning's incident would have convinced you that not following my orders is not only stupid but extremely dangerous." His hold on her arm tightened. "If you want to live, you have to trust me and do as I say."

Gillian was forced to admit she would already be dead if it wasn't for him. She drew a shaky breath. She'd been letting her emotions rule. Even worse, she'd sounded like a jealous shrew. If she ran now, she'd look like one, as well. "All right. But Evelyn's your problem." Again recalling how he'd tricked her, she added, "The two of you deserve each other."

With his free hand, he captured her chin, forcing her to meet his gaze. "I have no interest in Evelyn."

The heat of his touch traveled through her like a river of fire and she felt herself being drawn into the midnight blue depths of his eyes. Anticipation caused her breath to lock in her lungs.

"My only concern at this moment is keeping you alive," he finished gruffly, then, abruptly releasing her, turned away.

Watching him cross the room to the refrigerator, she fought to hold back tears of frustration. For a brief moment, she'd found herself actually thinking he might declare his love for her. Shock swept through her. Love! She'd used the word *love* in connection with Taggart. The man had played with her emotions simply to "cajole" her into behaving. I've written one too many romance novels, she chided herself.

All right, so maybe, even after he'd made a fool of her, there was a quirk in her chemistry that caused her to still be attracted to him, she confessed silently. But it wasn't love. He'd saved her life twice now. She saw him as her protector, her lifeline. When this was over, she'd be able to walk away without a backward glance.

Having had this little talk with herself, she concentrated on setting the table.

Chapter Ten

"I owe you an apology," Evelyn said, drying a dish and setting it aside.

Following dinner, Gillian had volunteered to wash the dishes and Evelyn had insisted on helping her. For the past few minutes, Gillian had been attempting to ignore her unwanted helpmate. Surprised by the honesty in the woman's voice, she glanced at her.

"I know I come on a little too strong sometimes. But I can't help myself. I like being the center of attention," Evelyn continued, a flush of embarrassment reddening her cheeks. "Usually my titillating banter gets a few laughs and some ogling looks from the men present." The flush deepened. "I know the women generally get a little piqued."

Gillian's first reaction was to say something soothing to ease the other woman's obvious distress. But Evelyn's outrageous flirting during dinner had been a strain on Gillian's control. She was in no mood to be diplomatic.

Besides, she reasoned, a sharp jab of honesty might be just what the woman needed. "You do make some very off-color remarks that can cause others to be uncomfortable."

Evelyn grimaced. "Tonight at dinner, I did just that, didn't I?" Without giving Gillian a chance to answer, she hurried on. "I know I did. Taggart smiled politely but the smile didn't reach his eyes. And Simon kept giving me disbelieving glances, as if he thought I must be a brick, or even two, short of a full load."

So that was what was bothering Evelyn. Gillian regarded her coldly. "You're worried about having lost your touch with men?"

Evelyn looked shocked. "Good heavens, no. Taggart and Simon are just a little too conservative for my current approach. I can adjust it a little and have them eating out of my hands."

Gillian had to give the woman high marks for ego. But then she'd seen Evelyn at work when the chestnut-haired beauty was serious about attracting a man and knew Evelyn had reason to have faith in her abilities.

Again, distress showed on Evelyn's face. "It's you I'm concerned about."

Gillian paused, soapy plate in hand, and looked at the woman. "Me?"

"I'm not good at being friends with other women. But I want us to be friends. My brother thinks the world revolves around you, and I'd do anything to please him."

"I can't fault you for your honesty, but you don't have to strain yourself," Gillian replied dryly. "Harold is a very nice man, but I'm not in love with him, and I've got no intentions of marrying him."

"Harold can be very persuasive. Once he sets his mind to something, he never admits defeat."

"Well, he's just going to have to settle for my friend-ship."

Unexpectedly, Evelyn smiled. "It's going to be fun watching him court you. You have no idea how charm-ing, how tender, how sweet he can be. He'll win." A coaxing quality entered her voice. "So how about us be-ing friends? Ida and I got along real well. Surely you and I can find some common ground. Say you'll try." A sad-ness suddenly shadowed her face. "The truth is, I miss Ida. She was the only real female friend I've ever had."

Gillian experienced an unexpected surge of sympathy for the woman. "I'm sure we can find some common ground." She didn't really believe this, but she'd said it and she promised herself she would try.

"And I'll forget about Taggart and Simon and put my energies into looking after you," Evelyn vowed.

Seeing an opportunity to rid herself of the woman's company, Gillian took it. "I'd really feel much better if you'd go back into town and stay there. Harold might never recover if anything happened to you."

"Nothing is going to happen to me." Evelyn's man-ner became motherly. "It's you we have to concern our-selves with, and I'm not leaving your side until this is over."

Mentally, Gillian groaned.

"Did you ever hear about the time Harold and I went picnicking in the Alps and he saved my life?" Evelyn asked brightly, as Gillian returned her attention to wash-ing the dishes. Without waiting for a response, she launched into a detailed rendition of the tale.

An hour later, Gillian stepped out onto the front porch and sank into one of the rocking chairs. Silently she vowed that if she never heard Harold's name again she would die a happy woman. Evelyn had gone from one story to another that centered around her brother and emphasized his virtues.

"Nice evening," a male voice greeted her.

Startled to have company, she glanced to her right to discover Simon coming around the side of the house. "Yes, it is." During the time he'd been there, she'd concluded that, like Taggart, he was a quiet man who preferred to keep pretty much to himself, so she was surprised when he sat down in the chair next to hers.

Setting his feet up on the railing and crossing them at the ankles, he leaned back and looked up at the night sky. "That friend of yours is a bit unusual."

"She's not a friend." Immediately Gillian felt guilty. She'd given her word she'd try to like Evelyn. "Well, not exactly," she amended.

Simon glanced toward her and raised a questioning eyebrow.

"It's a little difficult to explain," she hedged.

"Evening, brother. Evening, Gillian."

Gillian looked up to see Taggart approaching. Behind his polite expression, there was a chill in his eyes.

"Evening, Taggart," Simon replied in an easy drawl. He grinned at Gillian. "Looks like Taggart has come to take over here."

She caught an underlying innuendo in his voice that suggested he thought Taggart was a mite jealous at finding them together, but she knew better. Taggart's reaction was strictly a male territorial thing. He'd made her his concern, and he considered himself her primary protector.

Simon eased himself out of his chair. "Think I'll take another stroll around the perimeter."

Taking his brother's chair, Taggart assumed the same relaxed position. But his expression remained grim. "What happened between you and Evelyn in the kitchen? She's acting very peculiar. I expected her to be tagging after me and Simon all night. But she just informed me she's going up to her room to read, and she didn't make a single pass at me."

"Disappointed? Afraid she's decided that you're too shallow even for her?"

He scowled impatiently.

Silently she berated herself. That was a cheap shot. After all, she did owe her life to the man. "She's decided to concentrate on me . . . keeping me alive and being my best friend. As she put it, she'd do anything to please her brother." In fairness, Gillian added, "And she misses having a female friend. Ida was the only one of our gender I've ever known Evelyn to get along with."

"So now she envisions you taking Ida's place?"

Gillian signed tiredly. "Yes. I made it clear I'd never consider marrying Harold, but she believes her brother can accomplish anything he sets his mind to. She idolizes him."

Taggart turned his attention skyward. "Nice night."

"Yes, it is." Startled by this sudden change of subject, she studied his profile.

His jaw was set in a hard line. Suddenly grimacing in pain, he shifted his shoulder. The lines of pain lingered and he began to rub the side and back of his neck.

Unable to stop herself, Gillian rose and took a position behind his chair. He tensed with surprise as she began massaging his neck and shoulders. "Relax. I'm not after your body," she assured him dryly. "I just figure I owe you."

He said nothing but the muscles she was working on did begin to unknot. To her chagrin, she found the warm, hard feel of him beneath her palms stimulating. Embers of desire sparked to life within her. How could she still be so attracted to the man? she chided herself. She'd always been one to look beyond the physical in any relationship. So, maybe he did have some good qualities, she admitted. He was certainly reliable as a bodyguard. He was good to his dogs, too. And although he'd made a fool of her, he hadn't misused her.

Now it was up to her to see that she didn't make a fool of herself, she admonished, and ordered herself to go inside. But her legs refused to move. Her fingers kept working, and the embers became a fire.

"I'm going to check on Simon." In one lithe moment Taggart rose, breaking free from her touch. "Go inside but stay out of the living room."

For a moment she stood immobile, feeling deserted. Then came the sting of insult. Clearly, he found her unbearably boring. "I think I'll go to bed and curl up with a good book. It beats the company around here," she said haughtily.

Taggart's expression remained unreadable. "Go inside."

On the way upstairs, she frowned at herself. She knew where she stood with Taggart. It was childish of her to have lashed out at him. A flush reddened her cheeks. She'd sounded like a rejected lover.

"I will be so glad to be rid of that man," she muttered as she climbed into bed. His image filled her mind. Beneath her anger, an ember of desire sparked into life. Growling at her duplicity, she forced her concentration to the book she was holding.

* * *

Midmorning the next day Gillian stood at the bureau in her bedroom, looking down at her crystal lying on the polished wooden surface. Since rising, she'd managed to avoid Taggart almost entirely. Their paths had crossed only briefly in the kitchen when she'd gone in to get some coffee.

He'd been there with a younger man who bore a vague resemblance to the other Devereux men she'd met. This newcomer was introduced to her as Gyles Emery, a cousin of Taggart's. Gyles was a friendly sort with a pleasant laugh and a quick smile. She learned he'd arrived in the early morning hours to relieve Simon.

To her relief, Evelyn had still been sleeping and she'd managed to get back to her room and closet herself inside with the excuse that she was behind schedule on her book and should not be interrupted. And she had been working until her crystal had interrupted.

Yesterday the gemstone had proved to be too much of a distraction. It liked Simon but didn't like Evelyn. Gillian couldn't fault its taste, but the notes of discord it insisted on issuing when the woman was present had finally caused her to take it off and leave it on the bureau. She hadn't wanted to make the mistake of talking to it aloud in the presence of others.

Now a quiet, sustained, high-pitched note was coming from it. "Not imminent danger, but danger is very near," she muttered, trying to decipher the crystal's warning.

The tone mellowed slightly as if to say she'd guessed rightly.

"A lot of help you are," she grumbled. "I've known that for days now."

The crystal hit a sour note of indignation, then returned to emitting the quiet but sustained high-pitched note.

"I got your message," she assured it. "Now be quiet."

With a hint of sourness, it ceased.

A knock on her door caused her to jump. The gemstone issued a low, mellow sound and she knew without a doubt her caller was Taggart. "I've really got to work on your taste in men," she scolded the gemstone in lowered tones. "Clearly, all you care about is a great set of biceps."

Rewarding her observation with another sour note, the crystal fell silent.

A second, more insistent knock sounded. She was about to call out that she was busy and didn't want to be interrupted when the door opened and Taggart entered.

Earlier, she had paid as little attention as possible to him. Now she noticed how tired he looked, as if he wasn't sleeping at all. He closed the door securely, then moved toward her, coming to a halt only inches away.

Her crystal hummed a low, uneasy note.

"We need to put an end to this hunt," he said. "Preventing your death is not like preventing an accident. Each time I change the circumstances, I get an image of a new place and time."

A chill curled through Gillian.

"What I have in mind could be dangerous."

The thought of endlessly being pursued caused her back to stiffen with resolve. "Whatever it is, I'm all for it."

He nodded his approval, but the grim expression remained on his face. "Gyles and I are going to leave the house. When he sees me step out on the porch, he's going to come out of the woods and say he's been bitten by a rattler. I'll say that I have to rush him into town, leaving you and Evelyn on your own."

"Shouldn't Evelyn leave also?" Gillian demanded.

"You don't have to worry about Evelyn."

"I'd really rather she left," Gillian insisted. "In case you're wrong, I don't want her on my conscience."

"If I explained my plan to her, she'd insist on helping, get in the way and possibly get hurt. She's safest here, not knowing anything."

"Are you certain that isn't the male chauvinist in you talking?" Gillian asked dryly.

He captured her chin in his hand. "I need you to trust me and do exactly as I say."

The heat of his touch traveled through her, easing the chill of her fear. Deep within, a fire threatened to come to life. Silently she groaned in frustration. Neither her body nor her crystal seemed to understand that although she could trust him with her life, she would be an idiot to trust him with her heart. Stepping back to break the physical contact, she met his gaze levelly. "What do you want me to do?"

"I want you to act natural. Evelyn will think I'm leaving her as your sole protection. Let her think that. Before my truck is out of sight, I want you back up here in your room. You stay up here alone with the door locked for fifteen minutes. Then go down to the living room. Now repeat that."

"I come back up to my room as you pull away. I wait fifteen minutes, then I go down to the living room. That's it?"

"You wait *alone* with the door locked. Don't let anyone in, not even Evelyn. Have you got that?"

"I wait alone with the door locked," she repeated.

"That's it." Taking a step toward her, he cupped her face in his hands. "I promise you I will do everything in my power to keep you safe."

For one brief moment she was certain he was going to kiss her. Then, abruptly, he released her and strode out of the room.

Frustration mingled with self-anger. She'd wanted him to kiss her. "What I want is to be finished with this business," she corrected sternly.

Concentrating on his instructions, she remained at the ready by her door. She heard him descending the stairs and stepping out onto the porch. Immediately she heard Gyles's cries of alarm.

Dashing down the stairs, she nearly collided in the front hall with Evelyn, who came running from the direction of the kitchen.

Outside, Taggart had Gyles lying on the ground and was tying a tourniquet around his still-jean-clad calf.

"Shouldn't we slit his jeans, find the bite and cut little 'X's in the wound and suck out the venom?" Evelyn asked, peering down at the leg with unabashed interest.

"That's not always effective. I don't want to waste time. The tourniquet will slow the flow while I get him into town to the doc. He keeps a supply of antivenin on hand," Taggart replied.

"I'm sure you know what's best," Gillian said, hoping to cut short any further arguments from Evelyn.

"I suppose," Evelyn conceded. "I did hear it was best to get medical assistance as quickly as possible."

Using his body as a crutch, Taggart hoisted Gyles to his feet. "Gillian, get back inside," he ordered curtly.

"Yes, do get inside," Evelyn echoed. "I'll help get Gyles into the truck." As she spoke, she slipped under his other arm.

Entering the house, Gillian heard the truck door slam. This was followed by Taggart shouting commands to Evelyn to call Thatcher and have him send someone out. Next came instructions for her to keep the doors and windows closed and locked and to see that she and Gillian stayed inside.

Evelyn was shouting back assurances that she could handle the situation as he drove away.

Continuing to her room, Gillian closed and locked the door. Her crystal was pealing an alarm so shrill she could barely think. "Hush!" she ordered, glancing at her watch. It issued a final peal of alarm, then obeyed.

Taking a long, calming breath, Gillian then listened, trying to discern what was happening below. She expected to hear Evelyn making the call to Thatcher on the hall phone. But there was only silence. Fear for the woman swept through her.

Her conscience refused to allow her to rely solely on Taggart's word that Evelyn would be unharmed. Ignoring his instructions, she hurried to the stairs. At the upper landing, caution overpowered her panic. Maybe Evelyn had decided to check the doors and windows before calling the chief, she reasoned. She called out.

There was no answer.

Her panic returned. Warily, she continued down the stairs. The front door was still wide open. Standing to one side, she peered out. There was no one in sight but she could hear footfalls on the porch to the south side of the house. Unable to determine if they were Evelyn's and deciding it would be prudent to investigate before she called out announcing her presence, she eased out the door. Using the rocking chairs as deterring shields, she crouched low as she hurried along the porch. Reaching the corner, she peeked around it.

Evelyn was there, alone, frowning skyward.

Gillian breathed a sigh of relief. "I was worried when you didn't come back inside."

Jerking around, clearly startled by Gillian's presence, Evelyn's frown deepened. "You shouldn't be out here."

"Neither of us should," Gillian returned.

Evelyn nodded. "You're right." She made a shooing motion with her hands. "Let's get back inside."

As they entered the house, Gillian again glanced at her watch. She still had ten minutes before Taggart wanted her downstairs. "I'm going up to my room."

Evelyn caught her by the arm and jerked her around. "I've got too much to do, and I can't have you popping up unexpectedly, interrupting."

Gillian frowned in confusion. "What . . . ?" The palm of Evelyn's hand, open in the pose of a karate blow, struck her in the forehead. Releasing her in that same moment, Evelyn allowed the blow to propel Gillian backward against the wall. Stunned and with the wind knocked out of her, she began to sink to her knees.

"Come on," Evelyn ordered, again grabbing hold of Gillian's arm, this time to pull her roughly to her feet.

Gillian struggled, but the blow had left her dazed and her arms and legs refused to work in coordination.

"Behave!" Evelyn snarled, twisting Gillian's arm painfully upward behind her, then forcing her forward into the living room.

Taggart's prediction about which room she was going to die in was going to prove true, Gillian thought groggily.

"I can't kill you just yet," Evelyn grumbled. "That's going to be a little bloody, and I don't want to have to worry about leaving any blood smears while I finish my presentations."

Gillian tried to think clearly. Time. Evelyn was offering her time if she cooperated, and time was what she needed. She stopped struggling.

"That's better." Evelyn smiled triumphantly as she grabbed the cloth sashes used to tie back the nearest set of curtains. "Just this morning I was in a blue funk. I miss the ocean. I want to go home but I had to find a way to get you out from under Taggart's eagle eye long enough to finish you off." She forced Gillian to sit in one of the nearby straight-back chairs. "Then opportunity knocked."

Suddenly worried Taggart might not get back in time, Gillian tried to rise but continued dizziness from the blow made her slow and clumsy.

Evelyn jerked her back down and quickly secured her arms behind her. With the second sash, she tied Gillian's right leg to the chair leg. Then she proceeded to get a third sash and secure the left leg. "Now I've got to leave you for a couple of minutes and cut the phone line so Taggart won't have to wonder why I didn't call the police," she said, gagging Gillian with a fourth sash.

Alone in the room, Gillian fought against her bonds, but they held secure. Surely it had to be getting close to fifteen minutes since Taggart left, she reasoned hopefully.

"Handy little thing." Evelyn was grinning broadly when she returned. She held a small pocketknife up for Gillian to see. "It belonged to one of my former boyfriends. He gave it to me in gratitude for an exciting night. I always keep it with me." Her grin became playful. "And I'll bet, quick thinker that you are, you've already guessed I used it to put that little gash in your brake-fluid line. I've never been one to pass up an opportunity, and that cat provided a wonderful one." Her grin turned to a petulant frown. "Too bad it didn't work."

Gillian barely noticed the small knife. Her attention was on the butcher knife in Evelyn's other hand.

"Now this one..." Evelyn's smile returned as she pocketed the small knife and shifted her attention to the much larger one. "This came from Taggart's kitchen. I'm sure you recognize it. For my current purposes, it is much more functional." With the knife poised to strike, Evelyn took a step forward.

Frantically, Gillian struggled harder against her bonds. They continued to hold. Her grogginess gone, she tensed in preparation to defend herself. She doubted she could be effective, but still she refused to die without a struggle. When Evelyn got close enough, she would tip the chair and hope it knocked the woman down.

Evelyn stopped, grinned mischievously, then glanced at her watch. "We've got time for a little chat. I'll ungag you, if you promise not to scream. It would be useless anyway. No one could hear you. The only purpose it would serve would be to give me a headache and I'd have to kill you sooner."

Gillian nodded her agreement. Keeping Evelyn talking would buy time.

"I've tried but I honestly can't see what my brother likes about you." Evelyn's gaze traveled critically over Gillian as she approached and removed the gag. "Of course, I never really understood why he was so enamored of Ida, either. But he was. It would have killed him if she'd left him. That's why I had to make certain that didn't happen."

A cold chill curled through Gillian. "*You* had to make certain that didn't happen?"

"You don't really think that nerd Halley drove his car into her, do you? He worshiped her. He would never have harmed a hair on her head. That's why he had to die, as well. He'd have told the police he didn't do it, and he might even have been able to convince them to believe him. Besides, his death made a nice little package."

Bile rose in Gillian's throat. "You drove the car into Ida and me and then made it look as if Halley had committed suicide?"

Evelyn smiled proudly. "It took planning. I even had to spend some time with the guy, oozing adoration over Ida. He thought I'd introduce him." She laughed.

Watching her, Gillian realized the woman enjoyed killing. "Why me?"

"If you're asking about the hit-and-run incident, I simply didn't like you. I never have. Besides, Ida was always with someone. So, why not you? I certainly wasn't going to endanger my brother."

"Ida loved your brother."

"But she was getting tired of being under his thumb. I could see that."

"Ida was always willing to compromise. She and Harold probably would have worked out their differences."

Evelyn breathed an exasperated sigh. "The truth is, I was bored with her. It was time to get rid of her. She couldn't have children. That was fine with Harold, but it wasn't fine with me. I wanted nieces and nephews. I refuse to have children of my own. I know my limitations. I'd be a terrible mother. However, I'd make a wonderful aunt. I'd buy the little darlings presents and take them places. I'd be their favorite relative."

Evelyn laid aside the butcher knife and, taking one of the two pieces of rope that had been draped over her shoulder, she began twisting one of them tightly around her wrists. "When I noticed this out on the back porch yesterday, I just knew it would come in handy. A few nasty rope burns on my wrists, so deep they draw blood, should convince Taggart and the chief that I struggled valiantly to free myself in order to aid you. But, alas, I will have been too late. My wrists will be free but my legs will still be tied when Taggart finds me sobbing on the floor beside your chair. A moment later and I would have been able to fight for you, but…" She sighed with mock regret.

Keep her talking, Gillian ordered herself. "But why kill me now? I've done nothing to you and I certainly don't want to be a part of your brother's life."

"You really are dull-witted." Evelyn shook her head. "Harold wants you and he can be unbearably persistent. He'll waste time courting you when he could be producing my nieces and nephews. Even more, it's obvious you're attracted to Taggart. I couldn't bear to see Harold lose out to an unsophisticated hick."

"Taggart is not a hick." Gillian couldn't believe she'd said that. Her life was on the line and she was defending Taggart. She forced a nonchalance into her voice. "Besides, I have no designs on Taggart."

"That's just as well," Evelyn replied. "I doubt he'd ever give you a second glance."

That woman is really irritating, Gillian thought dryly.

"Convincing enough, don't you think?" Evelyn extended her bloodied wrists for Gillian's inspection.

Where was Taggart? Gillian wondered frantically. Don't panic, she ordered herself. Keep her talking. Appeal to her ego. "I never realized you were such a good shot with a bow and arrow."

Evelyn beamed. "I once dated a champion in the sport. He taught me. At the time I never dreamed it would come in so handy. I always like to learn at least one little something new from each of my men." Her smile turned to a frown. "Taggart must have ears like a fox. I still can't believe he knocked you out of the way just in time." She shrugged. "It was a good try, though. I'd have preferred a gun, but there's too much red tape involved. I was able to purchase the bow and arrows without raising an eyebrow. I said they were a gift for a special friend."

Gillian had a sudden inspiration. "There is one flaw in your plan."

Amusement glistened in Evelyn's eyes as if she found this declaration ridiculous. "And what is that?"

"You don't know who's been sending me the letters. If he gets caught, he'll tell the police he didn't kill me."

Evelyn laughed. "I'm not stupid. I wrote those letters."

Gillian stared at her. "But how . . . ?"

"How did I get them mailed from all those cities?" Evelyn finished asking the question for her. "Air travel is so very fast and convenient. I simply flew there and mailed them. Harold and our entire household staff are used to me keeping my own hours. If I miss coming home a night or two, they don't think anything of it, especially if I call Harold and tell him I'm working on a new program or I've found a new friend. They understand that I have to have my freedom in order to keep my creative juices flowing."

Everyone in the house other than Harold was probably relieved when Evelyn was gone, Gillian mused, but prudently kept this opinion to herself.

"Actually this little adventure has worked out wonderfully well," Evelyn cooed with pride. "For the past couple of years I've tried to convince Harold he should forget you, but when he told me several weeks ago about this business project he was developing in Boston, I knew I hadn't been able to discourage him. I knew he was simply finding a way to be closer to you so he'd have an excuse to pop by and see you. That's when I began working on my plan. By the time he gave me a definite date for the trip east, I was ready to set it into motion."

She picked up the knife again and grinned. "I covered my trail beautifully. I used cash and false names when I bought my tickets. No one ever asks for an ID when you pay with cash. And I wore wigs." Her grin vanished and her expression became businesslike as she again glanced at her watch. "It's my guess Taggart should be returning in about fifteen minutes or less, depending on how worried he is about you. Time to get this over with."

Gillian closed her hands firmly around the arms of the chair and prepared to lunge forward. The chair was heavy, but if she timed it just right she might be able to move fast enough to knock Evelyn off balance.

Suddenly a large male arm was being wrapped around Evelyn's shoulders while a hand closed around the wrist of the hand holding the knife.

"I think we've heard enough," Taggart said.

Evelyn screamed in rage, then began violently struggling for freedom.

Cursing under his breath, Taggart gave the wrist a twist, causing her to drop the knife. "Someone get her legs," he yelled. "She's got a kick like a mule."

Thatcher and Gyles both came rushing in from the deck.

"I thought you'd never get here," Gillian said shakily, when Evelyn was subdued and Taggart began to untie her.

"And I thought I told you to wait in your room for fifteen minutes," he retorted in an angry growl. "By the time Gyles and I met the chief partway down the drive and worked our way back here, you were already tied up. If she hadn't felt like talking, you'd have been dead."

"Did you hear much?"

"Nearly everything."

Gillian glared at him. "You were here all that time and you didn't even try to give me a signal? Do you have any idea how terrified I was?"

"I couldn't risk her seeing me. We wanted to get as much on her as we could."

Freed, Gillian started to stand. Dizziness threatened to overwhelm her and her legs felt like rubber. She sank back into the chair.

"She hurt you."

Startled by the fury she heard in his voice, Gillian looked up at him. It occurred to her that Evelyn was lucky to be in Thatcher's custody. The intensity of his anger caused hope to bloom within her. "She just stunned me. I really think what I'm feeling now is simply due to nerves. This has been a frightening ordeal."

Taggart scooped her up in his arms. "I'm taking you to see Doc Prescott."

She'd never felt so safe or so protected. "A person could get the impression you care."

"I do."

The honesty in his voice sent a thrill through her. Her head ached and she was still shaky from residual fear, but none of that mattered. The heat of his body was pervading hers, warming her and soothing her. Lying her head on his shoulder, she closed her eyes and allowed him and only him to occupy her mind.

"Are you feeling drowsy?" he demanded anxiously when they reached his truck.

"Comfortable," she replied in something close to a purr.

"Don't go to sleep," he growled. "You could be suffering from a concussion."

She smiled. "I like your concern."

His expression grim, he set her in the cab of the truck and fastened her seat belt. "I should have come up with a better plan. I could have gotten you killed."

"If I'd gotten killed it would have been my own fault," she assured him. "I should have stayed in my room like you said." A sudden thought crossed her mind. "Did you know Evelyn was the one who was trying to kill me?"

"I never saw your attacker, but you had said your crystal didn't like her and she had showed up very conveniently both times your life had been threatened. It occurred to me that she could be jealous of her brother's interest in you. I figured keeping her where I could keep an eye on her was the safest path to follow."

"I guess I should pay more heed to my little gemstone." Mentally, Gillian made a note to work on deciphering her crystal's moods more accurately.

"I wish you'd paid more heed to following my instructions," he grumbled worriedly. "I should have known better than to trust you to obey me."

She smiled crookedly. "I will next time."

"This is 'next time.'" His gaze bored into her. "Stay awake."

He looked so incredibly handsome when he was worried, she thought. Her mind was still swimming a little. Trying to focus, she found herself concentrating on his lips. "For a kiss," she bargained, then flushed at her forwardness.

For a moment he hesitated. Then, frowning indulgently, he cupped her face in his hands and kissed her soundly. "Now will you behave?"

She grinned impishly. "If you insist."

Shaking his head, Taggart rounded the truck, climbed in behind the wheel and headed into town.

Gillian lay in her bed at her grandaunt's house, frowning up at the ceiling. It was nearly noon the next day. She still had a minor residual headache, but other than that she felt fine...except for being overwhelmingly embarrassed.

Yesterday, when Taggart had taken her to Dr. Prescott's office, the doctor had concluded that she might have a minor concussion. However, he'd allowed her to go to her grandaunt's house with the stipulation that she was to be closely watched. She was allowed to sleep but had to be awakened every hour during the day and then every two during the night, and asked her name and where she was in order to determine that she was still fully cognizant of her surroundings. If she wasn't or if she became nauseous or developed any other symptoms, he was to be called immediately.

For the remainder of the day and evening and throughout the night, Taggart had been there. But he had not kissed her again nor whispered any sweet nothings in her ear. He had, in fact, been his usual stoic self. Gillian had accredited this reticent behavior to his being tired and worried.

Then this morning Dr. Prescott had stopped by to see her on his way to his office. He'd examined her, announced that she was out of danger and suggested she remain in bed the remainder of the morning, after which she would be free to resume her normal activities.

Fairly soon after the doctor had gone, Taggart had left also.

Gillian groaned and raked her fingers through her hair. Taggart had cared, but only because he'd felt she was his responsibility, not because he'd developed any tender feeling for her.

Her cheeks flushed scarlet as she recalled bargaining with him for the kiss when he'd sat her in his truck. And then there were those times in the night when he'd come in and woken her.

Remembering how she'd smiled seductively up at him caused her flush to deepen. She'd hoped he would kiss her again, but he'd remained stiffly formal. Now she was forced to face the truth. She'd made a complete fool of herself over the man again!

"I'll blame the concussion," she decided.

A knock on her door was followed by her grandaunt's entry.

"I was just getting up," Gillian said quickly, feeling guilty for having lain in bed so long.

"Taggart's in the living room."

Sitting on the side of her bed, Gillian silently groaned. "I'd really rather not see anyone other than you at the moment."

Wanda studied her anxiously. "Are you ill? Dr. Prescott said I was to call if you began to have any unexpected symptoms."

"No, I'm fine," Gillian assured her. "I simply don't feel like entertaining company."

"I doubt he's going to leave until he sees you." Wanda's voice took on a stern note. "Besides, you owe him a thank-you."

Gillian knew that determined look on her grandaunt's face. She also guessed that Wanda was right about Taggart. He was probably here to make one final check on her and then his conscience would be totally free. She might as well get this over with. "All right. I'll come down." Grudgingly, she shoved her feet into her slippers, then went to the closet to find her robe.

"Don't you think you should dress and fix yourself up a bit?" Wanda suggested.

Before Taggart's arrival, Gillian had been planning to do just that before she joined her grandaunt for lunch. But she didn't want Taggart thinking she cared how he saw her. "No," she said flatly.

Wanda frowned reprovingly. "I will never understand young people today."

A glance in the mirror caused Gillian to hesitate and reconsider at least brushing her hair. Then she remembered herself begging for a kiss and her jaw firmed with resolve. Relinquishing only to the point of combing her fingers through the wayward disarray to smooth some of the wilder tangles, she headed to the living room. From the hallway she could hear her grandaunt's crystals chiming cheerfully. They liked Taggart. Well, there's no accounting for taste, she thought dryly.

Taggart rose as she entered.

Startled by his appearance, Gillian came to an abrupt halt. He was wearing a suit and tie and holding a huge bouquet of red roses. "What—" she gasped out in confusion.

"I've come to propose," he said, approaching her and handing her the roses. "Figured I should dress properly."

Nervously her hand went up to her hair. Too late now, she thought. "Propose?" Distrust showed on her face. "You haven't acted like a man in love."

He frowned impatiently. "I have tried, several times, to explain to you that I had to concentrate on saving your life. From the first day I set foot in this house, I was drawn to you. I began to get a jumble of images when you were near. That had never happened before. But the image that was the most clear was the one of you lying dead. I realized the others were either wishful thinking or dependent upon my saving your life. But they were very... distracting. I began to be afraid that they would interfere with my ability to keep you alive."

A curl of excitement worked its way through Gillian. "Are you referring to the lecherous ones?"

"Those and others." He stroked her cheek gently. "Do you remember the cradle I was working on?"

His touch was disconcerting, making it difficult for her to speak. All she could do was nod.

"You asked if the pregnancy was in danger," he continued grimly. "It was. The cradle was for us. I couldn't stop myself from beginning work on it and yet I knew if I allowed myself to give in to the feelings I had for you, I could fail and lose you and our future together. I had to keep you at a distance."

She frowned at him. "You were certainly effective."

Frustration etched itself into his features. "It wasn't easy. I couldn't stop wondering what it would be like to kiss you. My desire to find out got so strong I used the flimsy excuse of a truce to satisfy it. That only made my staying away from you more difficult. Then Harold showed up and I became afraid of losing you before I had a chance to court you. It took all of my control to stop myself from throwing him out." A hint of embarrassment showed. "I was even jealous of your storybook heroes."

There was a heat in his eyes that was igniting a fire within her. Still, she wasn't going to trust him so readily this time. "You hid your jealousy well."

"I was trying to keep you safe the best way I knew how."

"What about last night? I was saved but you still kept your distance."

"I didn't want to spend the rest of my life being accused of taking advantage of you when you were in a weakened condition. When you agree to marry me, I want it to be with a clear head."

The embarrassment she'd been experiencing only minutes earlier played through her mind. "You can be a very frustrating man."

He regarded her coaxingly. "I'd hate to think the images I've been having all night are merely fantasies."

She wanted to be angry with him . . . to give him a taste of his own medicine. But she recalled the strain and anxiousness she'd seen on his face during the past days and knew that would not be fair. He'd suffered, as well. "Me, too," she admitted, allowing herself to be drawn into the midnight blue depths of his eyes. Moving into his arms, she added, "And I do want to thank you for saving my life."

"My mother would have been grievously disappointed if I hadn't," he said against her lips, playing with the beginning of a kiss as if wanting to savor the moment. "She paints portraits of all the members of our family, and she has yours already started."

Gillian recalled Taggart cutting his mother short. Now she realized that he had done that to prevent her from blurting out that Gillian was the right match for him. Suddenly she was being lifted away from him. "If you've come up with another reason to keep us apart, I'm throwing you out of here and barring you from ever crossing my path again,'' she threatened.

His gaze leveled on her. ''You've never actually given me an answer to my proposal. Will you marry me?''

She saw the worry in his eyes. That he was not taking her consent for granted endeared him even more to her. ''What woman could refuse her very own hero?'' A self-conscious smiled tilted one corner of her mouth. ''And just for the record, I have to confess, you did keep popping up in place of my fictional hero.'' Her smile warmed with purpose. ''Yes, I'll marry you.''

Drawing her into his arms, he kissed her as fervently as she'd described any of her heroes kissing their heroines. The crystals sang and a passion more intense than any she'd ever imagined possible awoke within her.

An image of herself, Taggart and three children suddenly filled her mind. Was she somehow seeing his vision of the future or was this merely wishful thinking? she wondered. Either way, she knew she would enjoy discovering the answer. Then everything but being in his arms was forgotten.

* * * * * *

COMING NEXT MONTH

Conveniently Wed: Six wonderful stories about couples who say "I do"—and *then* fall in love!

#1162 DADDY DOWN THE AISLE—Donna Clayton
Fabulous Fathers
Jonas's young nephew was certainly a challenge for this new father figure. But an even bigger challenge was the lovely woman helping with the little tyke—the woman who had become this daddy's wife in name only.

#1163 FOR BETTER, FOR BABY—Sandra Steffen
Bundles of Joy
A night of passion with an irresistible bachelor left Kimberly expecting nothing—except a baby! The dad-to-be proposed a *convenient* marriage, but a marriage of love was better for baby—and Mom!

#1164 MAKE-BELIEVE BRIDE—Alaina Hawthorne
Amber was sure the man she loved didn't even know she existed—until the handsome executive made a startling proposal, to be his make-believe bride!

#1165 TEMPORARY HUSBAND—Val Whisenand
Wade's pretty ex-wife had amnesia—and forgot they were divorced! It was up to *him* to refresh her memory—but did he really want to?

#1166 UNDERCOVER HONEYMOON—Laura Anthony
Pretending to be Mrs. "Nick" Nickerson was just part of Michelle's undercover assignment at the Triple Fork ranch. But could she keep her "wifely" feelings for her handsome "husband" undercover, too?

#1167 THE MARRIAGE CONTRACT—Cathy Forsythe
Darci would marry—temporarily—if it meant keeping her family business. But living with her sexy cowboy of a groom made Darci wish their marriage contract was forever binding....

SOMETIMES BIG SURPRISES
COME IN SMALL PACKAGES!

FOR BETTER, FOR BABY
by
SANDRA STEFFEN
(SR #1163)

A night of passion turned into an unexpected pregnancy for
Kimberly Wilson! So when Cort Sutherland learned he was a
daddy-to-be, he insisted on a convenient marriage. But with
vows exchanged, Cort and Kimberly realized they were still
almost perfect strangers! Could they live—and *love*—as
husband and wife before their bundle of joy arrived?

 "I do," the bride and groom said...without
love they wed—or so they thought!

Don't miss FOR BETTER, FOR BABY by Sandra Steffen, part of
the Conveniently Wed promotion, coming in July, only from

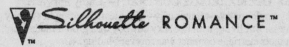

BOJ796

Conveniently Wed

"I do," the bride and groom said...without love
they wed—or so they thought!

Don't miss these six irresistible novels about tying the
knot—and *then* falling in love!

Coming in July, only from

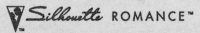

Silhouette ROMANCE™

**The wedding celebration was so nice...
too bad the bride wasn't there!**

Runaway Brides

Find out what happens when three brides have a
change of heart.

Three complete stories by some of your favorite
authors—all in one special collection!

YESTERDAY ONCE MORE
by Debbie Macomber

FULL CIRCLE
by Paula Detmer Riggs

THAT'S WHAT FRIENDS ARE FOR
by Annette Broadrick

Available this June wherever books are sold.

Look us up on-line at:http://www.romance.net

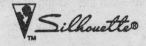

Silhouette®

™

SREQ696